Love is
a time of enchantment:
in it all days are fair and all fields
green. Youth is blest by it,
old age made benign: the eyes of love see
roses blooming in December,
and sunshine through rain. Verily
is the time of true-love
a time of enchantment—and
Oh! how eager is woman
to be bewitched!

NORA WAS A NURSE

Everything about Doctor Owen Baird interested Nurse Nora Courtney for she knew she was hopelessly and passionately in love with him. And when beautiful Lillian Halstead set her cap for the young doctor, Nora realised she must make him see her as a desirable woman as well as an efficient nurse.

PEGGY GADDIS

NORA WAS A NURSE

Complete and Unabridged

ULVERSCROFT
Leicester

First published in the USA in 1953 by
Modern Promotions, Inc.

First Large Print Edition
published November 1990

British Library CIP Data

Gaddis, Peggy
    Nora was a nurse.—Large print ed.—
    Ulverscroft large print series: romance
    I. Title
    813.52

    ISBN 0-7089-2316-X

Published by
F. A. Thorpe (Publishing) Ltd.
Anstey, Leicestershire
Set by Rowland Phototypesetting Ltd.
Bury St. Edmunds, Suffolk
Printed and bound in Great Britain by
T. J. Press (Padstow) Ltd., Padstow, Cornwall

For
SHERMAN

1

D R. JOHN COURTNEY came into the sunny, old-fashioned dining room, grinning with boyish glee and rubbing his hands together happily.

"This is the day!" he gloated exuberantly. "After today the old horse is going to shed his harness and start prancing. Who knows what may happen?"

Susan, his sister, her plain, scrubbed, unpowdered face touched with gentle amusement, said dryly, "Who knows, indeed? You've been my brother for a good many years and I'm very fond of you. Within reason, of course. I trust your discretion. Also within reason. But when a man your age who has been a country doctor for forty years suddenly is turned out to pasture and starts kicking up his heels, I fear for the future."

Dr. John glared at her, and Nora, fresh and pretty in her crisp white uniform, laughed at them both.

"Aunt Susie, stop low-rating the man I

love," she ordered sternly. "Grandpa is entitled to make a fool of himself at his age, if he wants to."

Dr. John turned his indignant stare upon her.

"Making a fool of myself," he snorted. "I ask you! My beloved family! The two females for whom I have slaved and denied myself for all these years; and you turn on me. A fool indeed! All I plan is a prolonged fishing trip in Florida. A *very* prolonged trip, I may add. I may even stay away until you two learn properly to evaluate my importance!"

Susan's sandy eyebrows went up in mock surprise.

"Oh, you're planning to be away permanently?" she asked innocently.

Dr. John glared at her.

"It's entirely possible," he assured her loftily.

Susan studied him thoughtfully, her graying head on one side, her eyes studying him.

"Well, you could easy as not get into trouble," she pointed out. "You don't look sixty-five. Strangers wouldn't take you for a day over sixty-four. You are reasonably well-preserved, not bad-looking, so you'd better be on your guard against predatory widows and frustrated old maids. You really are a rather attractive old coot."

"I wish I could say the same for you," snapped Dr. John.

Susan poured his coffee amiably.

"You could, easily, if you were as proficient a liar as I am," she told him placidly.

Nora smothered a laugh at the look of outrage on her grandfather's face.

"Now see here, you two," she ordered sternly. "Stop it this minute. It's disgraceful the way you snap and snarl and insult each other. Anyone who didn't know you as well as I do would think you loathed the sight of each other."

"Why do you think I'm going away on a prolonged trip?" demanded Dr. John.

"Out of the kindness of your heart to give me a vacation," said Susan, and exchanged grins with Dr. John.

"You two listen to me now, for a minute at least," urged Nora quickly. "Dr. Owen Baird is a complete stranger to all of us. Oh, you've met and talked to him, Granddad, when you went up to arrange for him to take over here. But you were on your best behavior, I know, and he probably thinks you are the traditional kindly, gruff-tongued but with-heart-of-gold old country doc. If he could hear you and Aunt Susie snapping and snarling at each other he'd begin to wonder if he hadn't suddenly stepped into some sort of madhouse."

Dr. John started to make an indignant protest, but Nora held up a silencing hand.

"Oh, I understand that when you two snap at each other and make cutting remarks it's only because you love each other and, for some crazy reason I never hope to be able to understand, you seem to be ashamed to admit it. Dr. Baird won't understand that, at least not until he's been here long enough to begin to get used to you; if he ever does, which somehow I doubt."

Dr. John set down his coffee cup so violently that some of the contents slopped over into the saucer, and Susan gave a disapproving cluck.

"Well, Dr. Baird is going to have just exactly two weeks to get used to *me*, because two weeks from today, I'm going fishing! If he can't take over my practise in two weeks, then it's going to be just too bad. I've got a date with a marlin, off the coast of Florida. And time and marlins wait for nobody!"

He looked from one to the other, and added fiercely, "And I haven't the faintest idea how long I'll be gone."

Susan poured a fresh cup of coffee for him.

"That means you may be gone as long as a week," she said placidly. "Almost that long, anyway. That will give me time to get the spring cleaning done."

And while Dr. John was struggling for a sufficiently cutting answer, the telephone in the hall shrilled loudly and Nora rose to answer it. She returned to give her grandfather the message, and went out of the house and toward the office: a small, tidy white frame cottage that faced the road, set beneath the shelter of friendly giant water-oaks.

Shellville had been a country settlement of only a few hundred when Dr. John and his bride had come there a little over forty years before, to the big old sturdy two-

5

storied house in which he had been born, and his father before him. It had then been the largest and finest house for miles around, an old ante-bellum plantation house. But hard times had befallen the plantation, and the land had been sold off until now less than ten acres comprised the entire estate.

Dr. John had built the cottage-office, and equipped it as a clinic, to which people travelled many miles over dirt roads that were passable only to strong mules or horses.

The years had been kind to Shellville, and it was now a modern, progressive small city boasting, according to the Chamber of Commerce, some twenty-five thousand. The road that ran in front of Dr. John's office-cottage was no longer a winding, narrow dirt road, hub-deep in mud in the winter, powdery with dust in the summer. Now it was a wide, well paved road and heavily travelled by motor vehicles of all kinds. Dr. John often wished that the cottage stood back from the road as far as the house did because of the noise of the traffic. But it brought him more patients, sometimes, than he wished for.

The location of Shellville, on the wide, lazy yellow river, had made it ideal as a textile site. Ten years before a New England firm had built modern brick buildings, surrounded them with neat, orderly rows of cottages for their employees. Now there was a pulp mill, a lumber yard, a plant for turning out the baskets and crates used by farmers who produced thousands of plants and seedlings for shipment throughout the country. But though Shellville had grown and prospered, with paved streets, an ambitious business section, street lights, water works and such, it was still a friendly, neighborly place, where people prided themselves on being "good neighbors" and knowing everybody in town.

Stretching away from the business section were the old-fashioned homes, neatly enclosed by carefully tended lawns and ancient trees. There were modern new homes, too, running largely to the "ranch-type" or "Cape Cod" beloved of newly married people.

But though Shellville had grown in all

directions and other doctors had come to start practise there, Dr. John's patients, their children and their children's children were loyal to him. And he had worked hard and faithfully for them.

From the time Nora, orphaned at the age of ten, had come to live with her grandfather and aunt, she had known that she wanted to be a trained nurse. Dr. John had been delighted. Secretly he had been relieved that she had not wanted to be "a female doctor," because he was old-fashioned enough to object to "women medics", though torture would not have forced him to admit it. He had seen her proudly through her nurse's training course at a big Atlanta hospital and had been touched and delighted when she had chosen to return to Shellville to work with him instead of choosing hospital duty or working in the office of some Atlanta doctor.

It was a peaceful morning in mid-March, which was spring in this south Georgia climate. There were a few patients already waiting on the big comfortable benches in the shade of the giant live-oaks with their long curtains of Spanish moss touched gently by the sweet, fragrant breeze. Beneath the trees the dying fires of azaleas, tall and lush-growing, just past their peak of bloom, lent a note of beauty to the scene.

Nora greeted the patients in her warm, friendly voice as she unlocked the outer office door. As they filed past her into the big, shabbily comfortable room, she saw that there were some she could attend herself, thus saving Dr. John's time. She changed the dressing on a textile worker's burned arm; gave a couple of injections; and by the time Dr. John came down for the beginning of office hours, only a few patients remained to demand his attention before he started out on his round of house calls and his visit to the neat county hospital.

Watching him as he climbed into his coupé a little later, Nora's heart was stabbed with the thought that he looked old and very tired. And she was deeply grateful for the knowledge that some time today a new young doctor was arriving who would shoulder much of the burden her grandfather had carried with such self-sacrifice and devotion for more than forty years.

She was working on the books when, shortly before noon, the door swung open and she turned to look up at a tall, young man with wind-rumpled dark hair, gray eyes set in a lean face that had not been exposed over-much to sunshine.

For a moment they were both silent, taking each other in. Nora sat where a bar of sunlight touched the warm chestnut-brown of her hair to an unexpected ruddiness. Freckles marched across her pert, tip-tilted nose and her eyes were golden-brown. In her crisp white uniform, the cherished, precious scrap of a cap perched airily atop her soft hair, she made a very pleasant picture which the young man seemed to relish.

"Well, hello, there," he greeted her happily. "I'm Dr. Baird. I believe Dr. Courtney is expecting me today."

Nora rose and held out her hand, her smile as warm and friendly as his.

"We're all expecting you, Dr. Baird, and with a great deal of pleasant anticipation."

"Well, thanks!"

His glance was so frankly admiring that the carnation color rose in Nora's face.

"Aunt Susie and I feel that unless he gets away for that fishing trip he's been wanting so long, she and I will have a nervous breakdown." She laughed hurriedly. "He's a lamb, of course, and we love him dearly. But he's overtired and not so young any more, and he desperately needs a rest. So right now he's a bit—well, let's be polite and say cantankerous, shall we?"

"By all means, let's!" agreed Owen cheerfully. "The work load carried by country doctors is killing. It's a wonderful break for me, being allowed to fill in for him while he is away, with the chance that if I do a good job, I may be allowed to stay on after his return and ease his work as much as he'll let me."

"We feel the break is on his side, Dr. Baird," said Nora impulsively. "To find a doctor with your qualifications who is willing to come to a place like Shellville, when there are so many richer and more varied fields open to ambitious men in your profession—" She broke off, unpleasantly startled by the odd, bitter smile that touched his mouth that was suddenly thin and taut.

"I didn't murder a patient in an absent-minded moment and have to take it on the lam and hide out here, Miss Courtney," he told her acidly.

The injustice of that brought a spark of healthy anger to Nora's eyes and her head went up.

"You know perfectly well that I did not mean to imply any such thing, Dr. Baird," she flung at him hotly. "If I seemed to, it was quite unintentional, I assure you. Your reasons for coming to Shellville are your affair and I have no desire to know them."

The door stood open, and before Owen could manage an answer, there were hurrying footsteps on the gravelled path and the door framed an enchanting vision. A girl not merely pretty but breath-takingly lovely, the sun like a spotlight on her honey-golden hair, on large deeply blue eyes set in a charming oval face, the warm red mouth carrying a wistful droop that was intriguing and touching all at the same time.

She looked shyly up at Owen, as he

12

stepped aside to allow her to enter, and her lovely eyes thanked him even as they took him in with a swift, comprehensive glance.

"Hello, Nora." Her voice was rich and sweet and held a touch of shyness as though she were fearful that she was unwelcome. "I came to pick up Uncle Dick's medicine. I didn't know you had company."

Impulsively, like a child, she lifted a dazzling smile to Owen and added, "Because I'm quite sure you're not a patient."

"Lily, this is Dr. Baird, who is taking over for Grandfather for a few weeks," said Nora, and tried hard to make her voice pleasant. "Dr. Baird, Miss Halstead."

Nora watched, wishing she didn't have to, for the expected look of amazed delight that always came over a man's face when he looked at Lily Halstead for the first time. As she saw Lily shyly put out her hand, and the eagerness with which Owen grasped it, Nora told herself acidly that it was a wonder he didn't fall flat on his face and grovel at the feet of this enchanting

13

creature. Why not? All other men seemed to!

"I'm so glad you're here, Dr. Baird," said Lily in that warm, slighly husky voice that added the last touch of charm to her very real beauty. "Poor darling Dr. John works so hard. But of course, he's the best doctor in the whole wide world, so naturally everybody wants him, so he has to expect to be overworked."

"I'm honored at being allowed to assist him," said Owen.

"I'm sure you are, because it really is a very great honor," and Lily gently, and turned to accept the bottle of medicine, still in its drug-store wrapping, that Nora extended to her. "Thank you so much, Nora. It was sweet of Dr. John to get it for us."

"How is your uncle this morning, Lily?" asked Nora pleasantly.

"About the same," sighed Lily mournfully, and lifted a brave, pathetic gaze to Owen and smiled faintly. "The only thing that seems to change is his temper. Usually for the worse. It's pretty explosive this morning, so I suppose I'd better get back and help Mother cope with him."

She divided an enchanting smile between Nora and Dr. Baird and went out, her exquisitely formed body in its crisp blue and white gingham moving with unconscious grace until she was out of sight. And not until then did Owen turn his bemused face to Nora.

"What an exquisitely beautiful girl!" he said dreamily.

"Isn't she?" Nora agreed politely, and turned away.

Owen was quiet and thoughtful for a moment.

"What's wrong with her uncle?" he asked after a moment.

"He's a paralytic," said Nora succinctly.

"And his niece is naturally very concerned."

"She's not really his niece," Nora explained, trying hard not to sound brusque. "Her mother is his housekeeper and has been since Lily was twelve. He won't have a registered nurse, so Lily has had the simple training necessary to look after him. Red Cross nurse's aide and what Grandfather and I have been able to teach her. She's a sort of nurse-companion-secretary."

Owen frowned angrily.

"What a perfectly rotten way for an exquisite child like that to have to live," he burst out.

Nora tried to bite back her next words but could not.

"Oh, I don't think she finds it so bad. Her family were textile workers, and Mr. Blayde is the chief stockholder in the mills. After her husband's death of pneumonia, Mrs. Halstead had to find a job to support herself and her child; Mr. Blayde needed a housekeeper and didn't object to Mrs. Halstead bringing Lily with her. If Lily's father had lived, she herself would be working in the mills now. I imagine she finds it much more pleasant living in Mr. Blayde's luxurious home and looking after him, even though he is cranky and hard to get along with."

She had tried hard to keep the sting out of her voice, but Owen's cold glance told her how poorly she had succeeded.

"Obviously you don't think very highly of textile workers," he commented dryly.

"That's not true," she flashed, and bit her tongue before more words could tumble out. It would be even worse to finish what she had almost said; that it was Lily herself whom she disliked and distrusted. Because if she did, Dr. Baird would think she was jealous of Lily's beauty. And what woman, seeing Lily, wasn't?

She looked up at Owen, met his cold, accusing eyes and said crisply, "If you'll drive up to the house, Aunt Susie will show you to your room and see that you are made comfortable. Grandfather won't be home until amost dinner time. I'm sure you will both have a lot to discuss then."

"Thank you," said Owen curtly as he turned and went out to where his new Ford coupé stood in the parking area.

She watched the car roll up the drive to the house, and her clenched fists were sunk deeply into the capacious pockets of her crisp uniform, and her golden-brown eyes were dark and angry.

She and Dr. Baird, she told herself dryly, certainly hadn't got off to a very good start, for two people who would be working so closely together while Dr. John was away. She had been startled by his unexpected reaction to her perfectly innocent surprise that a man of his qualifications should be willing practically to bury himself here; she supposed she had been impulsively frank, perhaps offensively so, in giving voice to that thought. It would not by any means be the first time she had blurted out some innocent, thoughtless remark that had had unpleasant repercussions. She was puzzled at his reaction, but she felt quite sure she could have aplogized and made him understand just how innocently she had spoken.

Lily's arrival, however, had forestalled any such attempt to clear the air between them. And after he had seen Lily—well, of course she should have known what to expect. Lily had that effect on men; they seemed to take one look at her and instantly fall under her spell. Unfortunately it was not an effect that wore off easily, either.

Nora had known Lily for a long time. She knew how cheap, how shoddy the real Lily was. But Lily was too smart to "let down" in front of any male, from six to sixty. Few men had ever really glimpsed the girl behind that dazzling façade of beauty and sweetness; to Nora, it was pose that only a fool could fail to see through.

Which, she reminded herself grimly, as she went back to work on the books, meant that ninety-nine per cent of the male population came in contact with Lily were fools! The thought made her murmur something under her breath that would have shocked Aunt Susie.

2

NORA and Owen did not meet again until dinner. Nora had come back after office hours, showered, changed into a yellow linen dress and tied a matching ribbon in her hair. She looked fresh and pretty and very attractive when she came down the stairs, and Owen, sitting with her grandfather in the living-room, looked faintly surprised at the sight of her, so changed from the crisply efficient office nurse.

But Nora coolly ignored him, so that her grandfather blinked, and went on out to the kitchen to offer her assistance to Aunt Susie and Cleo, the fat middle-aged cook who could do incredible things with a black iron frying pan and the most ordinary of foods.

"My land, child, you're wearing your new dress!" protested Aunt Susie artlessly. "You didn't have to dress up for Dr. Baird."

"Who dressed up for Dr. Baird?"

20

demanded Nora so belligerently that Cleo looked up from the Hollandaise she was carefully stirring. "I'm going to the movies with Jud, and maybe dancing later."

"Did you ask Jud to come to dinner?" asked Aunt Susie.

"Would you spank me if I did, but forgot to tell you?" Nora asked in mock terror.

"Naturally," said Aunt Susie placidly. "Don't I always beat you when you do such things? Whatever gave you the idea this was your home and that you were more than welcome to bring home a guest at the drop of a hat? It's not the way we've brought her up, is it, Cleo?"

Cleo chuckled richly and refused to be drawn in.

Aunt Susie, carefully lifting fresh asparagus from the boiling water, arranging it for Cleo's delectable sauce, asked lightly, "How did you like Dr. Baird? I think he's going to be quite an asset, don't you?"

"I think he thinks so." Once more Nora's irrepressible tongue and her impulsiveness made her speak her thoughts, rather than what was expected of her.

Aunt Susie stared at her, wide-eyed.

"You mean you don't like him? What's wrong? I thought he seemed very nice," she protested, puzzled.

"There's nothing wrong. Don't be silly. It's just that I really haven't had much chance to get to know him," protested Nora, flushed and badly at a disadvantage. "He stopped at the office, of course, but Lily Halstead blew in almost immediately, and Dr. Baird sort of melted and ran into the usual gooey consistency of men seeing the beauteous Lily for the first time."

Aunt Susie studied her for a long moment, and when she turned away, her eyes met Cleo's, wise and dark, and the two women exchanged an amused glance that would have infuriated Nora if she had seen it. But Nora had gone to answer the summons of the telephone and so missed that exchange of glances.

Jud Carter arrived just before dinner was announced, and offered breathless apologies for the narrowness of the margin.

"I was detained at the office," he said

cheerfully, and grinned disarmingly. "Very important case. Man accused of stealing chickens, and the court appointed me to be his defense counsel. Very important case; I may make the Atlanta newspapers with it, by my brilliant defense."

Jud was only an inch or so taller than Nora, and was inclined to put on weight. His face was round, fresh-scrubbed, cheerful, and his dark-rimmed spectacles gave him an owlish look. He and Nora had been friends since grammar-school days, and there was a sort of loosely knit understanding between them that some day they would be married. Nora was very fond of Jud. She rarely stopped to think whether or not she was in love with him. It would be years before they could hope to marry, for Jud was just getting started as a lawyer. His mother was a widow, and had lived frugally, with secret self-denial and sacrifices, to see him through his legal training. Until he was earning an income sufficient to take adequate care of her as well as a wife, there would be no thought of his getting married. All of which Nora knew and accepted quite simply, without being disturbed by it. If it ever occurred to her that hers was not quite the expected attitude of a girl in love and vaguely engaged to be married at some very future date, she brushed the thought aside. She was quite contented in her job with her grandfather where she knew she was doing a very necessary work; she loved the shabby, comfortable old house that was all the home she could remember. And years from now when Jud was established, his mother taken care of, they would be married.

Jud was pleasantly impressed by Owen, and the two men seemed to take an instant liking to each other. Dinner was pleasantly informal, the talk was amusing and interesting, and when the meal was over, and Jud and Nora were preparing to depart for the movie, Jud had an inspiration.

"Why don't you come along, Baird? Nora and I will be delighted to have you. Maybe Nora's got a girl-friend she can call and we'll make it a foursome," he suggested cordially.

Nora said quickly, "Call a girl fifteen minutes before show time, Jud darling?"

Jud said eagerly, "I bet I know a girl

who hasn't got a date and who'd be tickled to pieces to come along."

Owen was studying Nora coolly, and had not yet answered Jud's invitation.

"Who, for instance?" asked Nora, and to herself, As if I didn't know!

"Lily Halstead," said Jud, and added hastily, as he glanced guiltily at Nora and then at Owen, "Poor kid has a rotten time of it. Nurse to an old man who has a temper like a buzz-saw."

"I had the pleasure of meeting Miss Halstead this afternoon," stated Owen flatly. "It's a tempting invitation, but— thanks just the same. If I'm going to begin work with Dr. Courtney in the morning, there are no doubt many problems for us to discuss. Some other time, perhaps, if I may take a rain-check?"

"Sure, sure," said Jud hastily. "Nora and I will be delighted, any time, won't we darling?"

"Of course," said Nora smoothly.

"We must see to it that Dr. Baird meets a lot of our pretty girls," said Aunt Susie cheerfully. "A reception maybe, or some parties."

And though she hated herself for not

being able to keep still, Nora blurted, "He's already met the most beautiful girl in town. I'm sure the others would be an anticlimax."

Dr. John studied her curiously. It was unusual to hear that undertone of sarcasm in Nora's voice. Nora was the friendliest soul alive; she liked everybody. But apparently she and Baird had started off on the wrong foot, surmised Dr. John, and his jaw hardened. Well, if they had it wasn't going to keep him from his long anticipated trip. They'd just have to fight it out, one way or another.

He looked curiously at Dr. Baird. He seemed a nice, upstanding young man, and Dr. John was puzzled to understand why Nora should have taken a dislike to him. Ordinarily, as he well knew, Nora was as friendly as a setter pup. In his speculation he missed the finish of the conversation, and the next thing he knew Nora and Jud were going out to Jud's car.

Dr. Baird watched them go, and when the door closed behind them, he said involuntarily, "Why is it that every woman in the world has her knife out for a ravishing beauty like Miss Halstead?"

Susan eyed him curiously, amused.

"Instinct of the species, of course, Dr. Baird," she said lightly. "A girl who is just pretty resents one who is so beautiful that men fall for her in droves. I'm afraid Lily is not nearly as popular with women as with men, but then, that's understandable, of course."

Before he could manage an answer to that she went on briskly, "And now I'll leave you two to discuss matters far beyond the understanding of a woman like me."

As Jud started the car, he looked down uneasily at Nora.

"I was only trying to be polite to a stranger in our midst," he defended himself before she had time to accuse him. "Baird seems a right guy, and I thought it would be nice if he could get acquainted."

"Since he has already met Lily, and I might add, fallen flat on his face before her, your solicitude is a bit ill-timed," said Nora curtly.

"Well, Lily's not exactly the only gal in town," argued Jud.

"Really?" Nora's tone was one of mock surprise.

"Look," Jud was beginning to get angry, "why the blazes are all you gals down on Lily? Poor kid, she has a tough enough time—"

"*You* look." Nora drew herself up, and her tone was taut. "Haven't we had enough lightsome chatter about the fabulous Lily for one day? I certainly have, and I refuse to discuss her any more."

"Well, gee whiz," Jud was boyishly puzzled, disarmingly so, "I don't want to discuss the gal. It's just that every time her name is mentioned around women, the temperature does a dizzying drop. I just don't get it, that's all."

"Sorry, pal, I'm afraid I'm not in the mood to explain the facts of life to you at this point," said Nora sharply. "You might reason it out for yourself in an idle moment sometime. Women are never down on beautiful gals just because they *are* beautiful. There have to be other reasons."

"That's what I don't get, about Lily."

"And that, my friend, is what you'll never get from me." Nora's tone was warm and crisp. "It would do me less than no good at all to explain that women have an instinct about other women that is as sure as death and taxes. One woman can take a dislike to another, without reason; but when a whole crowd of women turn thumbs down on her, there are reasons plenty! But now if you don't mind, suppose we just forget about Lily and have fun, shall we?"

"Sure," Jud agreed, subdued, but his brow was still furrowed.

"If you're so mad about her," Nora hated herself for the words and the shrewish tone but could not control them, "why don't you marry the gal?"

Jud gasped in quick alarm.

"Good grief, I'm not mad about the girl; I'm sorry for her," he protested. "And the only girl I ever wanted to marry is you."

"Really?"

"Oh, come off that lofty peak of disdain, my good woman, and mingle with your betters." Jud's tone sought to be light but there was a tension to it that bespoke his anxiety. "You know how I feel about you, Nolly. How I've felt about you since you were six and I was eight and we met for the first time in Miss Logan's room at a dancing lesson—remember?"

Nora laughed.

"And you had to be forced, by a threat of a whipping, to ask me to dance with you, because you'd heard your mother saying what a 'cute couple' we'd make."

Jud grinned down at her warmly.

"She still thinks so," he told her happily. "And I couldn't agree with her more."

Nora put her hand on his where it rested on the wheel and smiled at him mistily.

"You're sweet, Jud," she said softly.

"And you love me?" There was anxiety in his voice.

For the first time, instead of an instant affirmative, Nora hesitated for just a moment, and then she said quickly, "Of course, darling, tons and tons."

Jud peered down at her anxiously in the thin light from the instrument panel, and suddenly one hand clenched and beat hard against the wheel.

"Darn it, if only some long-forgotten uncle in Australia or Hindustan would die and leave me his fortune!" He was still trying to sound mocking, but there was an undercurrent of deep emotion in his voice.

"Or some wealthy patient, without

friends or relatives, would take a sudden liking to me and remember me prominently in his will!" Nora said lightly.

"That wouldn't make any difference," said Jud sternly. "I refuse to live on my wife's wealth!"

Nora laughed aloud as he turned the car's nose into the parking space beside the theatre.

"Spurned again!" she mocked.

Jud switched off the ignition, turned swiftly to her, and with arms that would not be denied drew her close against him, and held her for a long moment before he bent his head and kissed her hard.

For a long moment she rested in his arms, and gave him back his kiss. And then she drew herself from his arms and turned her head away.

"We agreed that sort of thing was dangerously habit-forming, and to be indulged in on very rare occasions, remember?" she told him firmly, and slid out of the car and walked toward the entrance to the theatre, leaving him to follow her when he had locked the car.

3

THE next few days were busy ones, with Dr. Baird getting settled in his work, and with Dr. John freeing himself as fast as he could for the longed for fishing trip. Dr. John took Dr. Baird with him on his round of calls, and shared office hours with him, and saw to it that all the patients were convinced of Dr. Baird's complete understanding of their various cases and conditions.

Late one afternoon, when the last patient had been dismissed and Dr. John and Dr. Baird were relaxing over cigarettes, mulling over the day's cases, Nora was busy typing up cast-histories and getting files in order. She was absorbed in her task and not really listening to them, until suddenly she heard Dr. Baird speak authoritatively.

"I am firmly convinced, sir, that Mr. Blayde's condition is not really hopeless. I've told you about some of the techniques and the therapy used in such cases in the hospital. I believe that he can be given several more years, and without pain or helplessness. He seems completely resigned to the fact that he has only a few months to live; but, honestly, sir, I refuse to accept such a verdict for anybody! I'd like your permission to discuss a new system of treatment for him."

Nora, startled, looked up from her typewriter, and saw Dr. John glaring at the younger man, his eyes almost frosty beneath his bushy brows.

"Trying to show the old man up, are you, you young whipper-snapper?" barked Dr. John, and Nora held her breath fearfully.

Dr. Baird, apparently completely undisturbed, grinned.

"That's too ridiculous to merit an answer, sir," he said equably. "It's only that I've had the benefit of studying the very latest and most advanced techniques on certain heretofore, so-called hopeless cases of this kind. Naturally, you haven't. There's no reason why you should, since it would be out of the question for you to leave your practise here and spend months, perhaps years, in research and the like. I've just finished with such a training period; naturally, I look on all your patients with fresh eyes. You've been with them so long that you've been accustomed to their ailing conditions. I had no intention of being at all offensive, I assure you."

"Hadn't hey?" Dr. John was still frosty-eyed.

Dr. Baird said quietly, "I'm sincerely sorry if you find me so, Dr. Courtney. I had thought that what you wanted from me, as much as anything else, was a fresh approach to your practise. If I was mistaken, then I can only apologize and take myself off."

"Think I'd rather have my patients die because I'm a blundering old idiot, too stiff-necked to accept advice from a younger man, do you?" snapped Dr. John.

Before she could stop herself, Nora said sharply, "You know he didn't mean anything of the kind."

Dr. John flung her an angry glance.

"You keep out of this," he snapped.

But Dr. Baird smiled warmly at her and said, "Thanks."

"What was it you had in mind?"

demanded Dr. John, giving Nora a grumpy look as though affronted that she had sided against him.

Immediately Dr. Baird launched into a detailed and very technical analysis of the problem, outlining the treatment he planned, and Dr. John listened, his brows drawn together. Nora listened, too, not quite able to follow it all despite her nurse's training. But her mind was caught by the thrilling picture of a life that might be spared for at least a few more years, and when Dr. Baird had finished, she was flushed and bright-eyed with awed admiration. He smiled at her warmly, and then looked questioningly at Dr. John.

"You've seen this tried?" demanded Dr. John.

"Of course. I've assisted in such treatment, and the operation is a very simple one. Almost minor."

"And it has been successful?"

Dr. Baird hesitated a moment, frowning.

"In seventy-four per cent of the cases I've studied or worked on," he said at last.

"Then there is a margin for error?"

"Isn't there, in any medical case from measles to cancer?"

Dr. John got up and walked the length of the office, into the larger reception room, and back, one hand sunk deeply into the pocket of his shabby dark coat, the other rumpling his thick, snowy hair.

"We'll have to discuss it with Blayde, get his consent," he said at last.

Dr. Baird's eyes brightened.

"Of course, and that of his nearest of kin," he agreed.

"He has no nearest of kin," said Dr. John. "Swears he hasn't a living relative, and I suppose he ought to know. At least if he has, no one has ever come near him in the fifteen or more years I've known him. Mrs. Halstead and Lily look after him. I imagine they will inherit his estate, which is considerable."

Dr. Baird said lightly, "Well, if all goes well, it's going to be some time before anybody inherits his estate!"

Dr. John studied him curiously, his shaggy brows drawn together.

"You're pretty sure this thing will work, aren't you?" he demanded.

"I wouldn't have suggested it, sir, if

there had been any doubt of it in my mind," said Dr. Baird quietly. "Of course, in any case there are unexpected complications, but I'd say that there is at least a ninety to one chance of complete success."

"Dick Blayde was sixty-two his last birthday," Dr. John warned.

"Sixty-two is not old, Dr. Courtney. Not nowadays."

"You're darned right it isn't," Dr. John exploded. "I'm sixty-five pushing sixty-six, and I'm not an old man."

"I didn't mean to imply that you were." Dr. Baird's voice was slighly edged.

Nora rose and stood between them, her eyes dancing as she winked at Dr. Baird. Then she turned sternly to Dr. John.

"You're behaving like a nasty little boy who sees another boy coming on the playground with a newer baseball bat and glove than his," she said. "You're tired out and you're cross. Now behave yourself and go on home and rest awhile before dinner. You can discuss this later, after dinner, when you've had time to think it over."

To Nora's surprise, her grandfather assented to the suggestion and spoke in a bluff, off-hand tone that masked his embarrassment.

"The girl has some good ideas now and then. Sorry I went off the handle. It's just that it was a bit of a jolt to find myself making such a mistaken diagnosis. You're quite right, Dr. Baird. It takes fresh eyes to realize these things. And I need a refresher course in some good hospital, except they wouldn't let an old duffer like me in. See you at dinner." And before either of them could answer, he had marched out of the office and up the gravelled side path to the house.

Nora watched him go, and her eyes were misty when she turned back to Dr. Baird, who was watching her curiously.

"He's an old darling, but he is terribly tired and nervous," she began.

"He's the finest doctor I've ever worked with and I'm proud of the privilege," said Dr. Baird swiftly. "And thanks for taking my side in the argument."

Nora's color was high.

"I felt you were quite right," she told him primly.

"And thanks for that, too," said Dr.

Baird, and held out his hand. "Are we friends now?"

Nora managed a small, abashed laugh as she placed her hand in his.

"Of course, and I'm terribly sorry I've been such a nasty little twerp ever since you came," she blurted impulsively.

Dr. Baird laughed, his eyebrows raised slightly.

"Oh, have you been?" he asked teasingly.

"I deserved that," admitted Nora. "I deserve to have you think that I've been behaving in a perfectly natural manner. But from now on I'm going to prove to you that I *can* be—well, not quite so repulsive."

"You haven't been repulsive at all! What an idea! I just took it for granted you resented my coming in here and taking over for your grandfather," Dr. Baird assured her, and she discovered, her color deepening, that he still held her hand.

"I am very grateful you have come and I do want to be as much help to you as a nurse can be to a doctor taking over an unfamiliar practise."

"We both know that's very helpful indeed," said Dr. Baird, and his smile was so warm and friendly, the look in his eyes so admiring, that she colored more deeply and turned away hurriedly to her work.

That night after dinner, Dr. John and Dr. Baird went over the matter, studying Blayde's case history from the very beginning, and agreed that tomorrow morning they would visit Blayde together and outline to him what they had in mind, leaving the decision to him.

Nora saw them off on their morning calls, knowing that their first call would be at Blayde's, since it was the morning for an injection that Nora usually gave, but that this morning Dr. Baird would administer.

It was about eleven-thirty when the station wagon used by Blayde's servants pulled up sharply into the parking area beside the office, and Lily Halstead came hurrying in. There were no patients waiting, since it would be three hours before afternoon office hours began.

Lily was flushed, her eyes bright, and she was breathing hard. But it only accentuated her beauty as she leaned against Nora's desk, shaking a little.

"What the devil is this all about?" she demanded in a voice no man had ever heard her use. A rough, harsh voice born of rage.

Nora looked up at her coolly and wished some of the men who admired Lily so extravagantly, Dr. Baird for instance, could see her now, with her sweet, wistful mask down and the ugliness of her inner self showing so brutally plain.

"Just what's got you all wrought up this morning, Lily?" she drawled. "I haven't the least idea what you're talking about."

"Like fun you don't," snapped Lily, and made an abortive effort to pull herself together and to lower her voice. "I'm talking about this cockeyed idea this snoop of a Dr. Baird has of 'restoring' Uncle Dick to health!"

"And of course you are delighted at the thought," Nora said smoothly.

"Don't be funny!" Lily rasped hotly. "You know I've been counting the days until I can get my hands on the old devil's money. Mother and I are in his will for a whopping amount; and I need that money!

Dr. John has been telling us it was a matter of weeks, maybe a few months; and now this Baird creep comes along and says he can have several more years! *Years!* Why, I'll be old then. I may not be beautiful. I may be stuck in this hideous little fly-speck of a town the rest of my life!"

Nora, even knowing her well as she did, was sickened.

"He's been kind to you and your mother, given you a good home, more luxury than you ever dreamed of, and now you begrudge him a few more years of life?" she asked quietly.

"I want a few years of life myself," blazed Lily. "While I'm still young and beautiful. I want to go places, do things, be somebody. Why, with the money he has left Mother and me, I could go to New York, become a famous model, maybe marry a millionaire! But if he's going to live for years and years—why can't that Baird creep mind his own business and keep out of mine?"

Nora controlled her disgust with an effort.

"He's a doctor," she said thinly. "It *is* his business to help sick people get well."

"Oh, sure, sick people, but not like Uncle Dick," snapped Lily hotly. "Uncle Dick is old. He's lived a long time. Why should he want to go on living like he is?"

"But Dr. Baird can help him to live and to walk and have a normal life for several years longer."

Lily whirled upon her, hands jammed deep in the pockets of her simple but very becoming blue chambray dress, her eyes blazing.

"And what good is that going to do Uncle Dick? He'll die anyway. And it will just mean that I've lost valuable and important years out of my life," she raged. "I've looked forward to having that money he is leaving to Mother and me. It's maybe not very much just for me; but he will leave Mother a lot, and I can have that, and I'll be able to go to New York and have a lovely apartment and devastating clothes and who knows what could happen? But if that stinkin' Dr. Baird is going to start messing things up, it may be years and years and too late for the money to do me any good when I get it."

"I think," said Nora, trying to speak quietly, her voice shaking in spite of her efforts to control it, "that you are the most outrageous, the most thoroughly disgusting creature I have ever seen in my life. If some of the men who think you are so wonderful could see you, hear you now!"

Lily's smile was sweetly venomous.

"But of course they never will," she drawled confidently. "You're very good for me, Nora darling. You're the only person in the world before whom I can be really myself. Blow off steam, get it out of my system. And, of course, I can say anything I like to you, because you'll never tell on me."

"Won't I?" asked Nora evenly.

Lily's smile was mocking, derisive.

"Of course not. You're much to honorable and decent and fine to 'rat'." In Lily's tone the words were epithets of contempt. "And even if you *did* go against your high-minded principles and try to squawk it wouldn't matter, because any man to whom you tried to reveal the depths of my wickedness would only think you were jealous and spiteful and mean-minded. And he'd just feel sorry for me and more protective than ever."

It was true, of course. Nora had no argument against it, and knew the utter folly of attempting one.

"Did it ever occur to you, Lily, that most of the women who know you have your number?" she asked quietly.

Lily lifted her shoulders beneath the prim blue cotton frock and laughed.

"Oh, the women," she sneered, and her voice hardened. "I hate every female in this town. There isn't one of 'em that wouldn't knife me if she could; but she doesn't dare for the same reason *you* don't. And women never help another woman, anyway. It's the men that a girl like me has to depend on. And they are wonderful to me."

It was true, of course, but that didn't make Nora like it any better. For a moment the two girls sat eying each other, bitter enmity like a two-edged sword between them. And then a car drew up outside, and Nora glanced out of the window and drew a deep breath.

"Here's Dr. Baird now," she said

curtly. "Maybe you can talk him out of the new treatment for Uncle Dick."

She was startled at the change that came over Lily, though she had seen it often enough to have been prepared for it. Lily whirled, as the door opened and Dr. Baird came in. And then with a little broken cry she stumbled toward Dr. Baird and clung to him, while his arms went out instinctively to steady her, his startled face softening as he looked down at her.

"Oh, Dr. Baird, I've been waiting for you," stammered Lily, and her voice was such a broken mixture of fearful delight and anxious questioning that Nora blinked. "Is it true, Dr. Baird? Is it true? That darling Uncle Dick is going to have a chance to live?"

Nora sat with her eyes downcast, knowing what Dr. Baird would see in their depths if she met his eyes.

"We hope that it is true, Lily, we hope very much indeed that it is," he comforted Lily, who clung to him, weeping like a child, her face pressed for a moment against his shoulder. "You'd like that, wouldn't you?"

"Oh, of course, Dr. Baird, of course,"

Lily stammered radiantly, her flushed face lifted, tear-wet, her eyes shining. "Darling Uncle Dick has had such a terrible time. And he's been so good to Mother and me. Oh, it would be so wonderful! Almost too wonderful to be true!"

Dr. Baird patted her shoulder warmly, not *quite* as though she had been a child, and his eyes upon her were warm and deep with admiration.

"Well, we're hoping that it will be so wonderful it just has to be true," he promised her gently.

Lily drew herself reluctantly, with pretended shyness, from his arms, and scrubbed at her eyes childishly. Nora saw that the tears that had come so easily and so effectively had enhanced rather than dimmed her beauty.

"I'm sorry I went to pieces, Dr. Baird," she said humbly. "It's just that when I came home from doing the marketing, as I always do, and Mother told me about what you were planning, I couldn't believe it, so I rushed over here to hear from your own lips that it was going to happen."

Radiantly, as though he had placed in

her hands a gift so perfect that she scarcely dared touch it, she smiled at him. As Nora saw the bedazzled look in Dr. Baird's eyes something twisted at her heart.

"I'd better run along now," said Lily after a moment with a touching gesture of pulling herself together with a deep, hard, breath, like a child that has finished with tears. "Uncle Dick might need me, and I couldn't bear it if I were not there when he asked for me."

"I'll see you to the car. Sure you feel like driving?" asked Dr. Baird anxiously.

"Oh, I feel like flying now, with such a wonderful new hope for Uncle Dick," Lily assured him joyously, and with a single backward glance at Nora, her eyes blazing with triumphant malice, she walked out beside Dr. Baird.

For a long moment Nora sat quite still, staring straight ahead, her face set, her eyes hard. Lily wanted to be an actress, did she? Heck, right this minute she could take a scene away from Helen Hayes and make Helen look awkward. She drew a hard breath and her fists clenched tightly and there was an acrid, unpleasant taste in her mouth for which she could not account. Unless it was true that bitter hatred had an actual physical taste!

4

D R. BAIRD did not return to the office after the stationwagon drove away, and so it was not until dinner that night that Nora learned anything about the meeting with Dick Blayde.

"At first," Dr. John answered Aunt Susie's eager question, "he was inclined to scoff. Didn't believe it could be done."

Dr. Baird grinned ruefully.

"Well, naturally you can understand why he would hesitate to accept such a proposal from a Johnny-Come-Lately who had just arrived on the scene," he said cheerfully. "But once Dr. John convinced him it was possible, he became more interested. But he wanted to think it over, to have a few days to decide whether he wanted to go through the ordeal of the operation and the subsequent treatment. Think he will decide for it, Dr. John?"

"I believe he will," said John thoughtfully. "He has accepted the verdict of specialists that his condition is hopeless; I have to admit I accepted it, too. And frankly," he shot an unexpectedly stern glance at Dr. Baird, "I'm still not convinced that the specialists were all wrong, though by torture, I might be made to admit *I* was."

Dr. Baird grinned at him.

"The last time the specialists gave him a going over was two years ago, Dr. John," he pointed out firmly, but respectfully as behoved a young doctor speaking to an older one. "A lot of things can happen in and to a human body in two years. Certain nerves, muscles, organs can quietly re-build themselves to an unbelievable degree."

"I had suspected that," said Dr. John gently.

Nora sat quietly, listening to their discussion, grasping as much as her nurse's training would permit of the extremely technical and complicated process Dr. Baird was outlining; but her mind was really concerned principally with that ugly scene with Lily. If Dr. Baird had arrived a few minutes earlier and had just happened to step into the outer office, his presence unsuspected, what a jolt he would have got! But of course Lily's luck had held; that phenomenal luck that had made Lily such a controversial subject in Shellville since she was sixteen.

They were just finishing dinner when the phone rang and Nora answered it, to hear the voice of Jud's mother.

"Nora, dear, I haven't seen you in an age," said Marsha Carter in her soft, sweet voice. "Jud had to drive down to Jacksonville this afternoon and won't be home until later. I wondered if you wouldn't come over for a while so we could have a little visit."

"Thanks, Marsha, I'd love to," said Nora happily for she was fond of Jud's mother. "Be there as soon as I can make it."

She went back to the others and said lightly, "I'm going to run over and visit with Marsha for a while. I won't be late."

Dr. Baird rose instantly.

"Let me drop you off on my way in town," he suggested eagerly. "I have a sort of date."

"Well, thanks," said Nora, and felt oddly deflated, for no good reason at all.

"Jud will be back in time to drive me home."

The date, she told herself as she walked beside him out to his coupé, was with Lily. She was as sure of it as though he had said so, but after all, what business was it of hers? She was engaged to Jud, and that was that.

It was only a couple of blocks to the Carters' pleasant bungalow, and Nora thanked Dr. Baird almost curtly, as she got out of the car and turned toward the neat white gate.

"Shall I pick you up later?" he suggested, but there was a tentativeness about the tone that told her he wasn't quite sure how late he would be.

"Of course not." Her voice sounded curt and ungracious. "Jud will be back in plenty of time."

"I see. Good night, then," said Dr. Baird, and drove away, as she walked up the crazy-paved walk between beds of daffodils and narcissi, the velvety faces of pansies edging the beds.

Marsha was waiting for her at the door, and kissed Nora affectionately as she drew her into the house, chattering of her pleasure in this visit. Marsha was small and plump, still retaining some of the candy-box prettiness that had made her an acknowledged belle in Shellville for so long that she had not married until she was twenty-six. Her husband, ten years her senior, had adored her and treated her like a lovely, wilful child. Jud's birth had been a difficult one and they had been told they must have no more children. And so Marsha had lavished on Jud all the devotion of her loving nature. Jud's father had died when Jud was twelve and immediately Jud had become "the man of the family," taking over his father's loving duty toward the small, bewildered, grief-stricken widow.

Marsha's living-room was gaily feminine, almost fussily dainty, and there were times when Nora, looking about it, wondered how Jud felt about it. He must feel ten feet tall and awkward among so many delicate, useless, frivolous objects, she reflected.

Marsha said suddenly, when they had brought each other up to date about friends and acquaintances and local news, "You must be wondering, Nora, why I asked you to come here like this while Jud is away."

Nora looked as puzzled as she felt.

"I'm afraid I just thought you were lonely, and since we hadn't seen each other in a week or two—" she began.

Marsha leaned forward and patted Nora's arm affectionately.

"Well, of course it was partly that, Nora dear, but I've been wanting to have a serious talk with you for several months and the opportunity finally came about and I seized it."

"A serious talk with me? Goodness, Marsha, that sounds ominous." Nora laughed, but felt a faint touch of uneasiness.

Marsha was silent for a moment, obviously hesitant about what she must say, how she must phrase it. She sat in the gray-covered chair, her small, plump body in its neat blue linen dress held straight, one plump hand pleating the folds of her lavender-scented handkerchief on her knee, almost as though she were afraid to face Nora, to meet her eyes.

"Nora dear, you *do* want to marry Jud,

don't you?" Marsha said at last with an air of desperation.

Nora tensed ever so slightly, but answered lightly, "Well, of course, some day."

"I don't want you to wait for 'some day,' Nora; I want you to marry him now," said Marsha swiftly.

Puzzled, Nora said gently, "But, Marsha, that's out of the question. We can't possibly. There's my job with Grandfather, and then—"

"There's me," Marsha finished what Nora could not, or would not say. "The problem of what to do about me. I know that's the main thing that has kept you and my boy from being married."

"Why, what a silly thing to say or think, Marsha," Nora protested quickly and honestly. "That's not true at all. The problem of what to do about you is no problem."

"You're sweet, Nora." Marsha's voice was steady, though there was the faint threat of tears in her eyes. "You're both sweet, you and Jud. But it's a problem, just the same. I feel terrible to think that I'm keeping my boy from his happiness, the happniess that is any man's right, of marrying the girl he loves and establishing a home for her and for their children."

"Darling, you're being silly to worry about that," protested Nora warmly. "Goodness, I can't leave Grandfather, especially now that Dr. Baird is here and just getting acquainted and all. And Jud is just getting started in his business. Why, we've got years and years ahead."

"I wonder," said Marsha huskily, and Nora looked at her, unpleasantly startled. "So many things can happen, Nora. Life is so uncertain. You and Jud have been in love since you were children. You're so *right* for each other. And I couldn't bear it if something happened to break you up."

Nora stared at her, bewildered.

"But, Marsha, I don't understand."

"I didn't want to tell you, Nora, but after all, it's your right to know and I don't suppose anybody else would tell you," confessed Marsha miserably. "It's that Halstead girl, Nora."

"You mean Lily."

"Of course, the wretched girl!" Marsha's soft voice was brushed with anger. "She's the most shameless, depraved creature on earth, but how are you going to make a man like Jud understand that?"

"How are you going to make any man understand it?" Nora agreed bitterly. She had a fleeting picture of Dr. Baird and Lily together, and took time out to wonder why that bothered her more than the thought that Jud was seeing Lily.

"I'm going to tell you something that Jud probably hasn't told you, because he wasn't supposed to tell anybody," confessed Marsha, and looked uneasily at the door as though she expected Jud to be standing there looking at her accusingly. "Jud drew up a new will for Mr. Blayde recently."

Nora looked her surprise, and Marsha nodded happily.

"Jud was delighted that Mr. Blayde trusted him, of course, and Mr. Blayde has given him a few small jobs since. Testing him out, Jud thinks, and he has hopes that Mr. Blayde will be satisfied with his work and call him more often. Mr. Blayde's attorneys are in Atlanta, and now and then he wants somebody closer at hand. But you see, that's the trouble."

"I can't see any trouble in that," protested Nora. "It sounds pretty wonderful to me, and very encouraging for Jud. I'm awfully pleased."

"Oh, so am I, of course, if that was all," Marsha agreed bitterly. "But you see, I think Lily suspects that there was a new will and she's dying to find out about the legacy for herself and her mother, and she has been making a terrific play for Jud, hoping to get him to break down and tell her. Which, of course, he won't; only Lily doesn't know that. She's being so sweet and—well, provocative, that I'm worried Jud may make a fool of himself about her."

"Jud would never betray a confidence from a client," said Nora automatically, because she knew it was true, and she was still slightly dazed.

"Of course not," said Marsha scornfully. "You know that and I know it. The point is: does Lily know it? And the answer is that Lily can't conceive of any man being able to resist her to such an extent. There, as I see it, is the danger."

Nora looked at her in bewilderment, and Marsha's tone sharpened.

"That Lily, in her effort to find out about the will, is going to get Jud so crazy about her that he'll do something idiotic," she finished.

"Like throwing me over for Lily, is that what you mean?" asked Nora, and knew that it was. "Well, don't worry; Lily has her sights set on a much richer man than Jud."

Annoyed, Marsha nodded.

"I understand that, of course, but the question is, can she make Jud realize it, in time to keep him from being badly hurt?"

For a moment they studied each other.

"It's worried me a lot," Marsha said impulsively. "And that's why I thought if you and Jud were married now, instead of waiting, maybe for years, it would be better."

"If Jud doesn't care enough for me to be able to resist Lily's blandishments, or those of any other woman, I'd rather know it now than after we are married," Nora pointed out flatly.

"If you and Jud were married, no other woman in the world could have any effect on him, Nora, because he loves you very dearly," Marsha insisted. "It's just that waiting, stretching love so thin, and being lonely makes a man vulnerable."

Nora started to speak, but Marsha silenced her with a raised hand.

"Let me finish, Nora," she begged. "I've got some money saved up. It's a little over a thousand dollars, and I've been saving it in nickels and dimes and quarters, and a very rare dollar here and there, since Jud's father died. I knew that some time Jud was going to need it; I can't think of a time when he needs it more than right now, to make it possible for him to marry you. I don't suppose you like the idea of living here with me—no, no, let me finish, Nora dear. Any girl wants to set up housekeeping with the man she loves in a little place of their own, no matter how small it may be. But that takes money, and I thought if you and Jud could possibly be happy here, I could give you all of the house except my room, and honestly, Nora, I'd keep out of your way. I wouldn't be a nuisance."

There were tears in her eyes, though she was smiling tremulously, and Nora went swiftly to her and hugged her.

"You precious silly!" she scolded

fondly. "You a nuisance? You couldn't be, not if you worked hard at it and took lessons every day!"

Marsha brushed her handkerchief over her eyes and hugged Nora hard, almost with childish enthusiasm.

"I'm so glad, Nora dear," she said unsteadily. "I do so want to see you and Jud married and happy together."

"Not so fast, pet," protested Nora, and her brows were drawn together in a slight frown. "How do we know what Jud thinks about all this? Have you talked to him about it?"

"Of course not." Marsha was slightly shocked. "I wouldn't, until I talked to you. I had to know first how you felt. But of course Jud will be just tickled to pieces. He loves you very much."

"But not enough to keep him from being interested in Lily?" Nora's tone was slightly mocking.

"That's only because he is lonely."

"That's because she is exquisitely lovely and has a way of winding even the strongest man around her little finger, Marsha, let's face it," said Nora grimly, and thought of Dr. Baird rushing off to meet Lily.

Marsha sat silent for a moment, her plump, gentle face tired and her eyes touched with bitterness.

"Isn't it funny what utter fools men can be about a girl like Lily?" she sighed, and added honestly, "of course, I really have no right to judge her because I scarcely know the girl. But somehow I distrust and dislike her."

Nora grimaced.

"I know her very well and thoroughly despise her," she admitted frankly, and recalled the ugly scene in the office earlier in the day in which Lily had frankly revealed her inner self.

"I don't suppose you'd think of telling Jud the truth about her?" Marsha's tone made it a statement rather than a question.

"You know the answer to that, darling," Nora pointed out dryly. "He'd think I was jealous of her, which I am, and that I'm a no-good for trying to make things even more difficult for the poor dear child."

Marsha sighed heavily.

"It's really a problem, isn't it?" she sighed.

Nora grinned. "That may not be the understatement of the century, even if it does seem to be at the moment," she admitted.

She stood up suddenly and said briskly, "Well, I'd better be getting home. It's after nine."

"Jud should be home in another hour and he'll drive you," pleaded Marsha.

"Thanks, the exercise will do me good, and it's a lovely night," said Nora firmly.

Marsha walked with her to the door.

"You'll think over what I've said, Nora dear?" she pleaded.

Nora bent swiftly and kissed her cheek.

"Of course, dear, but after all, it's Jud who's going to have to decide," she said quickly.

"But if he asks you to marry him right away, you will?"

There was such eager hope in her tired eyes that Nora was very gentle. "I'll think about it, darling. That's the best I can promise right now."

"Well, I guess that's all I have any right to ask," said Marsha. "Good night, Nora dear, and thank you for coming over."

She stood in the lighted doorway until

Nora had reached the gate and turned to wave. And then the door closed and Nora walked on, her hands sunk deeply in the pockets of her light spring coat.

It *was* a lovely spring night, but there was a faint tang of chill in the air that made the coat feel welcome, and that made walking a pleasure. Nora had some hard thinking to do and she walked almost without awareness of the direction in which her steps were taking her.

She was puzzled because she had felt no lift of the heart when Marsha had pointed out that she and Jud could be married right away, instead of waiting for a year or maybe two until Jud had established himself. With the bits of business Dick Blayde was throwing his way, with the precious "nest-egg" Marsha had so carefully hoarded, and if Nora kept on with her job, as of course she would for a year at least, there was no reason at all she and Jud could not be married now instead of later.

Why, then, was she completely unexcited about the prospect? She and Jud had known for years that some day they would be married; they had planned and talked and yearned toward that day. Yet now when it could be upon them if they wished, she felt no elation whatever. Instead, she was finally forced to admit to herself, she felt even a trace of panic that slowly crystallized into a definite unwillingness! She didn't want to marry Jud!

The realization brought her to a halt and for a moment she stood quite still, startled, wide-eyed. She looked about her to discover that she was now several blocks from home, going in the opposite direction. As she turned her steps back toward home, she tried to analyze the sudden feeling of not wanting to marry Jud that had swept over her. It was so crazy! Why, she couldn't remember a time since she was sixteen when she hadn't looked forward to marrying Jud! She had taken her nurse's training in Atlanta, and Jud had taken his law degree at Emory University. They had been on the same campus, but they had not seen a great deal of each other, because their hours were so different. But they had looked forward to her infrequent days off when they could be together. They had planned endlessly and happily toward the day when they would be married; and now when the day could be upon them, she wanted to turn and run the other way just as fast as she could!

They had rarely been separated for more than a few days, a week or two at most, since they had been school children. She was fond of Jud. The rather startling thought occurred to her that maybe just being fond wasn't enough. And yet they had all the things marriage counsellors felt were so important on which to establish a happy and well-adjusted marriage: similar tastes, similar background, mutual interests, mutual friends. Life with Jud, as his wife, would be pleasant, safe, peaceful; but was that all she had the right to expect from marriage? Where was the magic enchantment, the rapture, the glory of love that people wrote songs and poems and books about? She liked Jud's kiss; it did not disport her into ecstasy. But, she wondered warily, as she reached home at last and went up the walk, maybe that sort of thing only happened in books and popular songs and poems. She couldn't know, of course. But something deep within her seemed to flash a tiny, warning bell. It could be true, and somewhere there could be a man who could show her that it *was* true! The thought startled her and she tried to put it away from her, as she let herself into the house and went up to her room, careful not to disturb Aunt Susie and Dr. John, who were already in bed.

5

SHE was alone in the office the next morning. Office hours were over for the morning and Dr. Baird and Dr. John had departed on the morning round of calls, when the telephone rang sharply and Nora took up the receiver.

"Is that you, Nora?" said Dick Blayde's dry voice. "Would it be possible for you to come over for a little chat? I know you are alone in the office at this time, but I really want very much to talk to you. I thought perhaps Miss Susan might answer the telephone while you are away, and I promise not to keep you long."

"Of course, Mr. Blayde," said Nora instantly. "I'll be right over."

"Thank you, Nora, I'll appreciate it."

Nora put the little sign "DOCTOR IS OUT: WILL BE BACK—" and set the hands of the little clock at 11.45. She carefully locked the inner office and left the reception room door open, and hurried up to the house.

"Aunt Susie, I'm running over to Mr. Blayde's; will you look after the telephone until I get back?" she called, rummaging in the desk drawer for the keys to the elderly sedan Aunt Susie used for marketing and her own junketing about town.

"Of course, darling," answered Aunt Susie, and added anxiously, "is it something serious? Mr. Blayde isn't worse?"

"I don't think so. He just said he'd like to talk to me," answered Nora, and hurried out.

The Blayde home was a handsome, stately affair of yellow brick set in the midst of two acres of carefully tended lawn and gardens. The door was opened to her by Mrs. Halstead, a neat, tidy woman in a crisp percale house-dress beneath a snowy white apron. Her prematurely white hair was brushed straight back from her angular face, and Nora reflected briefly, as she always did, that Lily must have got her sensational beauty from her father, for there was no trace of it in her mother's anxious, care-worn face.

"Good morning, Nora," said Mrs. Halstead anxiously, and ushered Nora across the wide reception hall to the down-stairs suite that had been made over for Dick Blayde when he had had his first stroke of paralysis. "Mr. Dick's waiting for you."

She opened the door, and Nora caught the sound of Dick's angry voice, and of Lily's subdued accents. Then Mrs. Halstead announced Nora, and Dick dismissed Lily savagely.

As Lily brushed past Nora, she said under her breath, "He's all yours, the old so-and-so, and I wish you luck with him."

Nora went on across the handsomely furnished sitting-room to the bedroom, where Dick Blayde sat in a wheelchair beside a window open on the garden. He was thin, gaunt, his face etched with lines of suffering that were almost as much mental as physical, for Dick Blayde had not taken kindly to helplessness. His thinning hair scarcely managed to cover his pink dome of a head, and his eyes were faded and bitter. Yet they warmed as he saw Nora, crisp and fresh in her white uniform and cap.

"Good morning, Nora," he greeted her

with honest warmth in his voice. "It was good of you to come."

"If you need me, Mr. Blayde, I'm always glad to come," said Nora quite honestly. "What's wrong?"

"Oh, nothing so far as my miserable physical condition is concerned," said Dick bitterly. "But then a tree or a stone doesn't suffer physically, and that's about all I am these days."

He motioned her to a chair drawn up near his, and Nora dropped into it and waited. Dick shot her a stern glance, and his jaw hardened.

"What do you think of this Baird that Dr. John has taken into the office?" he shot at her so unexpectedly that Nora felt her face grow warm.

"He is a thoroughly competent doctor, Mr. Blayde. He comes very well recommended and his qualifications are high," said Nora quickly.

"Oh, I'm quite sure Dr. John would check on him thoroughly before he'd trust his practice to him." Dick dismissed that as of little consequence. "I was asking what you think of him as a man."

"I'm afraid I wouldn't know too much

about that, Mr. Blayde," admitted Nora frankly. "After all, he's only been here a short while, less than two weeks, and of course he's been very busy getting settled and meeting the patients and so on."

Dick grinned, an unexpected grin that was rather touching on his stern, thin-lipped, bitter mouth.

"So you won't talk, eh?" he said teasingly. "All right, let's put it another way. What do you think of this operation and treatment he wants to try out on me, to prolong my worthless life a few more years?"

Nora was startled, puzzled.

"I'm a nurse, Mr. Blayde, not a doctor or a surgeon," she pointed out. "The whole thing is too much for me to be able to understand or properly evaluate. Grandfather seems to think it would be successful, or he would never have permitted Dr. Baird to suggest it to you."

Dick turned his thin, gaunt face toward the window and looked out with unseeing eyes at the garden, glowing with springtime beauty in the bright warm sunshine.

"I like Baird; instinctively I trust him," he said at last slowly. "And of course I have the utmost confidence in Dr. John. But I wonder if it's worth it. I'm tired, Nora; I'm an old man. I wonder if it's worthwhile to go through the trouble of an operation, perhaps a painful convalescence. I'm a coward about pain, Nora, all men are; don't let them kid you! All for just another year, maybe two or three, of life not much less restricted than what I have now."

"Dr. Baird feels that you would be much less restricted, that you might even walk again, and that you could have several years more of life," Nora pointed out gently.

"Then on the other hand, as he was honest enough to admit, the whole thing might be unsuccessful and I'd be right back where I am now, or perhaps even worse."

He was not looking at her. She had the feeling that he had forgotten her presence; that he spoke his thoughts aloud, turning them over and over in his mind, bringing them out into speech, studying them, voicing them merely to make them clearer to himself.

"I won't take the risk," he said so

suddenly, so sharply that Nora almost jumped, and his clenched fist beat a hard blow on the arm of the chair. "You can tell 'em for me, Nora, that I've decided against it. I'll go on as I am and hope they're right when they say it won't last more than a few more months, at most."

"But, Mr. Blayde—"

"My mind is made up, Nora," he cut her off brusquely. "Look at it from a sensible viewpoint; what has life given me up to now that is so precious I'd fight to hang onto it? I'm a lonely, embittered old man. I was too busy making a fortune when I was young to 'waste' time finding a woman I could love, marrying, bringing up a family. Now I've come to the end of the trail and somehow, whatever may lay beyond intrigues me more than what I might gain by a few more years of life. No, I've made up my mind. We'll leave things the way they are. Tell Dr. Baird for me, will you?"

"Of course, Mr. Blayde," said Nora, and after a moment she asked uneasily, "but are you *quite* sure, Mr. Blayde?"

His smile was quick, warm, almost without the bitterness she had always seen twisting his mouth since the first time she had seen him.

"I'm quite sure," he told her, and added quietly, "tell me, Nora: if you were in my place, wouldn't you feel the same way? Be honest with me, Nora, wouldn't you?"

Nora looked at him for a long moment: his gaunt, twisted, all but helpless body; his tired eyes; his haggard, pain-etched face. And suddenly it seemed to her a terrible thing that anybody should want to prolong a life that had so little of warmth or tenderness or love in it.

"Yes, Mr. Blayde," she said softly. "I think I would."

He held out his hand, and when she put hers in it, he smiled up at her, that singularly sweet, unfamiliar smile.

"Thank you, my dear, for your honesty," he said quietly. "I think you are the most honest person I've ever known. I honor and respect you for it. May I offer you a bit of advice?"

"Of course, Mr. Blayde, I would be grateful."

"It's just this, Nora. Don't let your profession blind you to the fact that the greatest happiness the world can offer anyone is love and companionship. In being a fine nurse, don't forget that being a fine wife and mother is an even greater profession. And then when you get old and tired, you'll not be alone and empty-hearted."

There was the sting of tears in Nora's eyes, but she smiled at him warmly.

"Thank you, Mr. Blayde," she said softly.

Dick studied her for a moment, and his gaunt face was more kindly than she could ever remember seeing it before.

"You and Jud Carter," he said after a moment. "You think well of him, don't you?"

"Oh, yes," said Nora quickly.

"So do I," said Dick. "He's got good stuff in him. Don't wait too long before you marry him, Nora."

Nora's color was high, and her eyes were warm and soft.

"I'll remember, Mr. Blayde," she said at last.

As though suddenly he had tired, he said brusquely, "Well, run along now. Thank you for coming over."

"I was glad to come," Nora told him

gently. "I'll always be glad any time I can be of service, though frankly I'm afraid I haven't been much, today."

"There's where you're wrong, my dear," Dick assured her promptly and not merely as though he were being polite; he spoke with vigor and conviction. "You've been of great service and I'm grateful."

As Nora came down the stairs, Lily came out of the big drawing-room, moving with swift furtiveness as though she did not want to be seen by the servants or her mother, and came close to Nora and walked beside her to the door. There, with another glance over her shoulder, she bent until her face was very near Nora's.

"Thanks, pal," she murmured softly. "I won't forget it."

Nora drew back, puzzled, annoyed.

"I don't know what you're talking about," she said curtly.

"About your persuading dear, darling, sweet Uncle Dickie-love to pass up Dr. Baird's treatment," said Lily sweetly, and laughed at the startled, indignant look on Nora's face. "I was listening outside the door, of course. Isn't that what anyone would expect of a low creature like me? So I know, and thanks a lot."

And without giving Nora time to marshal her anger so that she could frame an indignant response, Lily danced back through the drawing-room door and out of her sight.

Nora's eyes were blazing and her mouth was taut as she got into the elderly sedan and jammed her foot hard on the starter. It was, as Lily had said, only what one might have expected of her: that she would eavesdrop and spy and twist what she heard to fit her own plans and purposes. And Nora's heart was bitter with loathing for the girl, who looked like a sweet, demure little angel and who was, in reality, a young devil!

Late that afternoon, when office hours were over and Dr. John had already gone up to the house to have a brief nap before dinner, Dr. Baird came out of the private office to the reception room where Nora was working on the books.

She was, as always, instantly and sharply aware of his presence, but she kept her head bent above the work she was doing until the last entry had been made.

And then she looked up to see Dr. Baird leaning against the big old-fashioned table in the center of the room, his arms folded, his eyes on her with a curious look that puzzled her even while it brought the color to her cheeks.

"So you persuaded Mr. Blayde not to take the chance of prolonging his life for a few more years," he said quietly at last.

Nora caught her breath. So Lily had lost no time getting in her ugly licks!

"I did nothing of the sort," she protested hotly, but Dr. Baird ignored the protest.

"I'm a little curious," he admitted, as though she had not spoken. "Curious as to whether your attitude means you lack confidence in me."

"I did not persuade Mr. Blayde to do anything at all," she told him hotly. "He telephoned and asked me to come over. I went, of course. After all, he is a patient whom Dr. John has been treating for years. He talked about the operation, the treatment, and suddenly he said that he didn't feel it was worth an operation and the long, probably painful and tedious convalescence, just to get a few more years of life which he hadn't found so gay that he cared about prolonging it."

Dr. Baird was still studying her with that curious, enigmatical regard that made her angry and that for some queer reason she was unwilling, or even unable to explain, also hurt.

"Lily repeated the entire conversation to me," he said evenly.

"Lily would," growled Nora deep in her throat.

"She is naturally interested, because she is fond of Mr. Blayde. She is grateful to him, and she is anxious for him to live longer, and to be more comfortable. That's understandable, isn't it?"

Nora, remembering the morning when Lily had burst out with savage fury to express the fear that Dick Blayde's life might be prolonged, set her teeth hard. It would be less than no good at all to try to convince Dr. Baird of that scene; he would have had to be a witness to it to believe it. And of course Lily would always be wary enough and shrewd enough to see that no man ever caught her in such an evil mood.

Nora said quietly, "If Lily eavesdropped, as she must have done, because

Mr. Blayde and I were alone throughout the conversation, she evidently misunderstood. I gave Mr. Blayde no advice whatever; I'm a nurse, not a doctor. I haven't the remotest idea what the results of the new treatment might be. But I have confidence in your ability and in your integrity and I know you would not suggest such a course unless you were pretty sure it would be successful."

"Thanks," said Dr. Baird in a tone of surprise. "Then if you feel like that, why did you persuade him—"

"I persuaded him of nothing," she said hotly. "He asked about you, what I thought of you as a doctor and so on. I told him what I have just told you. And then he seemed to think about it."

As concisely as she could she repeated to him the entire scene between herself and Dick Blayde, not knowing whether he would believe her or not; too angry, too hurt to care very much. When she had finished, Dr. Baird nodded slowly.

"I see," he said at last. "And I can understand how Lily read things into the scene that weren't there. It's easy to realize how she could misunderstand."

"She didn't misunderstand," flashed Nora rashly. "She merely twisted the scene to fit her own purposes."

And then she could have bitten her tongue out, but it was too late. The ill-tempered words had been spoken, and she all but held her breath for Dr. Baird's blast of outrage and defense of Lily.

"Loving Mr. Blayde as she does, almost as though he were her father," he said slowly, thoughtfully. "I can see why she would be frightened of his taking such a chance. Because, of course, it *would* be a chance. I feel he could be reasonably sure of a seventy-five-twenty-five chance of complete success. But that's about as much as any doctor can guarantee in a case of serious illness."

There was, Nora told herself bitterly, no answer she could make to that. None, at least, that would be acceptable to Dr. Baird!

"Naturally, I'm disappointed," admitted Dr. Baird. "Mr. Blayde's condition is a challenge; I think any doctor would feel that challenge. Any illness or injury is a challenge to a doctor. I feel that Mr. Blayde himself would be benefited and we might add some small measure to the field of knowledge about paralysis. But of course, if he is unwilling to go through with it, that's that."

The telephone on Nora's desk rang and she picked up the receiver with a hand that shook slightly. Dr. Baird waited to see if it was a patient. When he heard her greet Jud warmly, he turned and went out and she could see him going up the path to the house.

"Hello? Nora?" Jud repeated, and she came guiltily back to the realization that he had said something she had not heard.

"I'm sorry, Jud. Dr. Baird was just leaving the office," she stammered. "I didn't hear what you said."

"I said that I was sorry I didn't get back from Jacksonville last night in time to drive you home," said Jud. "Marsha tells me you two had quite a gab-fest."

"I suppose you might call it that," Nora agreed cautiously, wondering just how much Marsha had told him.

"Well, how's for going to the dance with me tonight and then you can tell me all about it?" suggested Jud cheerfully. Without waiting for her to answer, he went on, "I'll collect you about eight-thirty, shall I?"

"That will be fun," said Nora, and tried hard to make her voice warm and gay. But after she had put down the telephone, she sat for a long moment, her mouth drooping, her eyes fixed on a space as though her thoughts were a confused and not too happy jumble.

6

ONCE a month the American Legion threw open its comfortable quarters for a dance to which the members were allowed to invite guests who were not members. It was a high spot of the month to those of dancing age—which, in Shellville, meant nearly everyone—because there was a good local orchestra, there was a buffet, and one was sure that the party would be a gay, but not wild one. Mothers were quite willing that their daughters should attend, and quite sure that they would be well looked after by the group of carefully selected chaperones.

Tonight the place was well filled and Jud and Nora were dancing their third dance, when Nora looked up and saw Dr. Baird and Lily coming in. She set her teeth hard and almost missed a step, but receovered before Jud could realize it.

Lily was exquisite, as she always was. Her ruffled pale blue organdie had a snugly fitted bodice, and modestly rounded neckline and a full billowing skirt that all but brushed the tips of her silver slippers. Nora, knowing that Mrs. Halstead's loving, patient fingers made every stitch of her daughter's clothes, eyed the many narrow picoted ruffles that comprised the billowing skirts and had a stab of pity for the woman who must have worked long, long hours on the delicate frock.

"Oh-ho," said Jud, as he saw the two in the doorway, Lily smiling shyly, sweetly up at Dr. Baird, whose handsome dark head was bent attentively toward her. "Our new Doc is stepping out tonight. And in charming company. Wonder how that happened?"

"What's to wonder about? He's a man, isn't he? And Lily is lovely-looking," said Nora curtly.

"Sure, Lily's a doll." Jud agreed a trifle more warmly than Nora felt was necessary.

Dr. Baird laughed at something Lily had said, and held out his arms to her. Lily slipped into them with an unconsciously deft movement, and the next moment they had joined the dancers already filling the smoothly waxed dance-floor.

Nora was popular, and before she and Jud had made the length of the floor, someone had cut in. The next thing she knew, a few minutes later, Dr. Baird was smiling at her, tapping her partner on the shoulder and taking Nora into his arms. Nora looked swiftly about and saw that Jud was dancing with Lily.

"Quite a nice party," said Dr. Baird lightly, and laughed at Nora. "Oh, don't look so disapproving. I left word with Miss Susie where I could be found if needed."

"I wasn't disapproving at all," protested Nora, and wondered furiously how it was seemingly always possible for this man to put her on the defensive, if not actually in the wrong. "I was delighted to see that you were having fun. Why shouldn't you?"

Dr. Baird's grin was a trifle tight.

"Look, Nora," he said unexpectedly, "I don't know what it is, but you and I seem to snap at each other every time we're off duty. Is it something I do that ruffles your feathers? I've always been able to get along with people. Even nurses who dislike me."

"That's absurd. I don't dislike you," Nora told him swiftly.

He looked down into her eyes, and there was a probing look in his own.

"Don't you? Well, I'm glad to hear it. With Dr. John leaving day after tomorrow, it's nice to know that you and I are friends, at last," he told her lightly.

The dance ended in a blare of sound and the dancers milled about, laughing and chattering. It was obvious that Dr. Baird had made friends in the town, for he was greeted warmly, introduced about, and drawn immediately into the circle. Jud and Lily approached—hand in hand, Nora noted, and reminded herself not to be a fool—and as they joined the circle about Dr. Baird the atmosphere chilled very slightly. But not so slightly that Dr. Baird was not aware of it, and Nora saw the angry gleam in his eyes as he claimed Lily for the next dance.

Jud, claiming Nora, said, "Lily sure can dance."

"Lily's quite accomplished," said Nora colorlessly.

Jud's jaw set.

"It's the darnedest thing why all the gals

in town seem to hate that poor kid!" he burst out. "She's like a kid at the circus for the first time tonight. She's really having fun. But every time the women look at her they give her the 'deep freeze' treatment. Is it because she's from the wrong side of the tracks? Are they still holding that against her, for Pete's sake?"

Nora said mockingly, "You poor sweet! Don't be an idiot. Lily's too beautiful, too completely devastating for any woman to trust her."

"Is that really it? They're jealous?" asked Jud, puzzled.

"Well, partly, anyway," Nora contented herself with saying, wondering as she had wondered so many times in the past how a man could be stupid enough not to see beneath the surface of Lily's beauty to the character behind it.

It was almost eleven when Dr. Baird received a telephone call, and Lily was left standing alone near the doorway while he went to take it. Jud instantly drew Nora over to join Lily, and the three stood talking, Lily looking up at Jud with such gratitude that Nora was touched in spite of herself. Lily had hated standing there alone and she was deeply grateful to Jud and Nora for joining her.

Dr. Baird came back, saying quickly, "It's an emergency. I'll have to leave immediately."

"Shall I go with you, Doctor?" The words came instantly to Nora's lips, spoken out of her nursing experience.

"Thanks, that won't be necessary, Nora," said Dr. Baird, and smiled warmly at Lily. "I'm sure Lily won't mind showing me the way to the Ferguson place, though I could probably find it myself. And if it's too late when I've finished there, I'll take her on home. If not, we'll come back here."

"It's the Ferguson baby?" asked Nora anxiously.

"Yes," said Dr. Baird. "The mother was terribly alarmed, but I'm hoping that she is exaggerating. Mothers often do. Sorry to drag you away, Lily, but if you don't mind helping me to find my patient?"

"Of course, Owen," said Lily eagerly, and it may have been only to Nora that there seemed the faintest possible emphasis on the use of his given name. "I wouldn't want to stay here a minute without you."

To Jud and to Nora she said sweetly, dewy-eyed, "Thank you for being so kind to me."

Jud and Nora watched them hurry out, and then Nora looked up at Jud, startled to see the white line of anger about his mouth.

"You just can't bear to be separated from him five minutes, can you?" he said through his teeth, and Nora could only stare at him, round-eyed with astonishment. "Come on. Let's get out of here. I seem to have lost my taste for dancing, too."

"You're being absurd," she stammered.

"Am I?" His grasp on her hand was so strong that she could not withdraw it without a struggle and had to walk with him out of the hall and down to the parking space where his car waited.

As he got in beside her and started the car, Nora put her head back and laughed aloud. Jud flung her an angry glance.

"What's so funny?" he growled as he turned the car away from town and speeded up.

"You are," she told him frankly. "Pretending that you lost interest in the dance just because Dr. Baird left. As if you didn't think I had brains enough to realize that it was Lily's departure that made you suddenly want to go home."

"That's not true and you know it," he told her angrily. "Standing there where a whole raft of people could hear and crying out, 'Shall I go with you, Doctor?'"

Nora sat up and looked at him, no longer amused, no longer mocking. Now a healthy anger shook her and her eyes were hot.

"May I draw you a diagram, please?" Her voice had a cutting edge. "I am a nurse; Dr. Baird is Grandfather's substitute. Dr. Baird is a stranger in these parts. The Fergusons live in a rather isolated section that is difficult to find at night, even for people who are more or less familiar with the section. The Ferguson baby is very frail and has had measles. The doctor was 'emergency.' As a nurse, I felt it my duty to accompany him to be sure he found the place without delay and perhaps to be able to help him when he got there."

93

Jud growled, "Well, it didn't sound that way. It sounded as if you couldn't bear to be separated from him for five minutes."

Nora studied him for a long moment, and then she sighed and shook her head sadly.

"What's it all about, Jud?" she asked quietly. "You want to fight with me and you're hunting for an excuse. But do please find one that makes a little sense."

In the thin light from the instrument panel of the car she could see his set, grim face and suddenly he brought the car to a halt on the shoulder of the road and switched off the ignition.

"Why should I want to fight with you?" he asked curtly.

"You tell me," she invited.

"I don't want to fight with you, Nora; what a silly thing to say. It's just that it made me so darned mad to see you yearning to run away from the dance with your precious doctor," he began defensively.

"The truth is that you couldn't bear to see your precious Lily leave with him, isn't it?" she asked sweetly.

"Now what do you mean by that?"

"Oh, skip it," she said harshly, and added quietly, "did Marsha tell you what she and I talked about last night?"

He was silent for a moment, hesitant, and then he said reluctantly, "Well, yes, she did."

"And?" she probed gently.

"And she said that you hadn't made up your mind whether you wanted to marry me or not," he added sulkily.

"But you have?"

"Look here, Nora, why do we have to growl and snap at each other like this, instead of discussing things quietly and calmly?"

"You started the growling, remember? You snapped first and I defended myself. Any jury would render a verdict of self-defense."

"You know darn well I want to marry you, Nora," he told her sulkily. "It's just that we decided to wait until I was a little better established. Marsha's savings would melt like snow if we tried to jump the gun."

Nora laughed. It was not a merry laugh. It was little more than a gust of mocking sound.

"This is the point where I'm supposed to return your ring, isn't it?" she mocked him bitterly. "But since ours was just 'an understanding' and not a formal engagement, and since I haven't a ring to return, all I can say is the understanding is at an end as of now. And if you don't mind, I'd like to go home."

"Nora, don't be like that!" he protested, but to her suddenly sharp ears the protest was half-hearted and she thought she detected a note of something very near relief. "You know I didn't mean that. It's just that—well, Marsha doesn't understand. We couldn't possibly accept that money from her, knowing how slowly and painfully she managed to accumulate it and that it must be untouched, for her own use if anything should happen to me."

She had to admit that was true. She knew that she would never have accepted Marsha's offer. Then why was she feeling hurt and resentful and jilted!

She drew a deep breath at last and said evenly, "You're quite right, Jud, of course. I never for a moment intended to accept the gift. I know as well as you do that we have no right to be married now, and I think it would be the smart thing just to admit that it's not at all likely that we'll ever be married."

"Oh, now, wait a minute," he protested sharply.

"This 'understanding' business is pretty silly, anyway, Jud," she went on as though he had not spoken. "It's really a sort of habit we've gotten into. We've known each other since we were babies; propinquity, isn't that what they call it? Just drifting along, concentrating on each other, until now we don't even know whether we are in love or not."

"But, Nora," he protested.

"No, wait, Jud. It's a rather startling thought for both of us, I know. But let's face it. Ever since we were children, we've taken it for granted we were in love and that some day we would be married, so we've never given ourselves a chance really to discover whether it's love or just habit! Let's start all over again, Jud. You date wherever you please, even if it's Lily; I'll do the same. And then if, some day we find we still want to marry each other, we'll be *sure*."

He was silent for what seemed to her a

long time, and then he asked curiously, "You're not sure now, Nora?"

"Are you?" she demanded flatly.

Once more he was silent, and suddenly Nora laughed gently.

"You see, Jud?" she pointed out. "We've taken it for granted, but we've never really stopped to analyze it. I'm very fond of you, Jud. You're fun to be with; we have mutual friends, mutual interests. And yet there is enough difference between us for us to be able to argue about things. But is that love?"

"Sounds like a darned good substitute," he growled, bewildered and resenting his inability to understand what she was driving at.

"But that's just it, Jud. A substitute!" she pointed out eagerly. "Who wants a substitute when maybe the real thing is available? We might be married and have a long peaceful life together, and never really *know* whether it was really love or just habit."

"Would that be bad?" He was still puzzled and annoyed, but her keen ear caught what she was now certain was a touch of relief in his voice.

"It would be if ever, after we were married, either of us met somebody and discovered the difference!" she said swiftly. "Jud, I've never thought much about it until now. I suppose I was busy learning to be a nurse, and that's a very absorbing thing, my friend. And I was so used to the thought that some day you and I were going to be married that I never paid much attention to other men I met. But somehow, Jud, lately, I've begun to wonder if maybe you and I might not be taking a chance by not—well, looking around a bit before we take the leap. Maybe somewhere there's a girl who could make you feel the way popular songs, stories, poetry say love makes a man feel when he meets the One Girl. Maybe there's a man somewhere who could make me feel like 'Sweet Alice, Ben Bolt'— 'weep with delight' when he gave me a smile and tremble with fear at his frown. That sounds corny, I know, and I wouldn't hurt your feelings for the world, Jud, but honestly, whether you smile at me or frown at me doesn't make a whole heck of a lot of difference to me!"

Affronted, he snapped, "Well, thanks a lot!"

She turned her head, smiling at him.

"Be honest, Jud," she entreated. "Would you feel like going out and committing suicide if we had a terrific quarrel and I said I wouldn't ever speak to you again?"

"Of course not. I'd know you didn't mean it and that we'd patch things up again."

"So you'd just grin and wait?"

"The grin wouldn't be a happy one, but I guess that's about it. You see, Nora, I know you so well."

"That's just the point, Jud. We know each other so well that we can anticipate what's going to happen. That's what comes to people who have been married for years; somehow I don't believe it's part of what people mean by being 'madly and gloriously in love.' There just has to be something else besides what you and I have."

Jud was studying her, puzzled, annoyed, offended. Suddenly he put out his arm, drew her hard against him and kissed her full on the mouth. Nora lay unresisting against his shoulder, examining the kiss in her mind, and then she sighed, shook her head and drew back.

"You see?" she asked quietly.

"See what? You're the darnedest girl!"

"No reaction! Kissing me was not too much different from kissing Marsha. It didn't have any *zing!*" she told him mercilessly.

She heard him swear under his breath. Somehow she had to make him understand how she felt.

"Jud dear, when you kissed me, did you feel any glow, any excitement, any emotion that—well, like the song says, 'When you're in love, you're nine feet tall'? Did it make you feel as though you could go out and play mumblety-peg with man-hole covers?" she demanded, so much in earnest that in spite of himself Jud chuckled.

"It didn't make me feel like Super-Man and all his cohorts, if that's what you mean," he admitted dryly.

"That's exactly what I mean," she told him eagerly. "When you kiss someone you love enough to want to marry, there is supposed to be—oh, star-dust and moon-silver and the fragrance of a thousand unknown flowers and the tingling of tiny golden bells."

"Look, baby," Jud's tone was condescending, amused, no longer annoyed, "you've been reading a book! You've got yourself all mixed up and confused. You're talking about physical attraction, something that burns itself out into ashes in less than no time at all. What you and I have is a basis for a good, steady, well-adjusted marriage. The other is dangerous stuff to fool around with and can get you into a peck of trouble."

"Then I want to get in trouble," she told him absurdly. "I want to know that I'm really in love, Jud, not just getting married because I'm so used to the man I drifted into it. So let's forget the understanding, Jud. Let's start all over again. Let's have occasional dates as good friends; but let's date other people, too, and, sort of prospect around. Then if we find that we really *do* want each other, we'll know it's for keeps."

There was a moment in which he was silent and thoughtful. And then he asked quietly, "Is that really what you want, Nora?"

"Don't be hurt or annoyed with me, Jud. It really is," she told him honestly.

He raised his hand in a little gesture of defeat and resignation.

"Then, if that's the way you want it, that's the way it will be," he said after a moment. "The lady must always have her way in affairs of the heart—it says here."

"You're a darling to understand, Jud," she told him with quick relief.

"Who understands?" he protested. "I'm just going along with a gag."

"Well, thanks anyway!" she told him happily. "And now I think I'd better go home. It's late and I have to be up at seven, all bright-eyed and steady of hand."

Jud nodded and drove on to where he could turn the car and headed back to town. On her door-step, he took her hand, bowed low over it and said with a mock-tremble in his voice, "Good-night, Miss Courtney—*may* I call you Miss Nora? Don't think I haven't had a most illuminating evening. When may I see you again?"

Nora laughed, but entered with spirit into the moment.

"It's been charming, Mr. Carter, perfectly charming," she assured him sweetly. "I'm a very busy gal, with a date for every week-day night. But you might ring me some time soon and I'll see what date I can break for you."

Jud drew her unexpectedly into his arms, held her close and hard and kissed her with vigor. She was a trifle breathless when he released her, and Jud was perfectly aware of it.

"No reaction, huh?" he crowed triumphantly, and strode down the walk to his car.

Nora grinned as she let herself into the house and crept quietly up the stairs to her room. At the head of the stairs she saw that the door to Dr. Baird's room was open, and in the corner beside the window, the moonlight sifted over his untouched bed.

She had a quick, startled feeling of anxiety. The Ferguson baby! She went on slowly, sobered, to her own room, her mind brushing anxiously over all the many complications that could have resulted from the baby's attack of measles. For a healthy, normal baby measles was serious enough. But for a baby less than a year old, as frail and as weak as the Ferguson child, measles could easily be fatal. And at the word she shivered, remembering Mamie Ferguson who had had "bad luck with her babies," losing three in infancy. Her whole heart had been set on this one, and Mamie could not have another child. If only, Nora told herself drearily, she could have gone with Dr. Baird, to see for herself—And then she pulled her thoughts back sharply. Dr. Baird was a thoroughly competent doctor and quite capable of handling the situation without the assistance of a nurse. And it had been completely, almost embarrassingly obvious that he had preferred Lily's company to hers!

She made herself undress and go to bed, but she was still wide awake when Dr. Baird's car came into the drive and she heard his cautious footsteps on the stairs. She turned her head and looked at the luminous dial of the small clock on the bed-side table. A quarter past two, and

Dr. Baird and Lily had left the dance at eleven!

She couldn't stop herself. She slid out of bed, swiftly wrapped her blue tailored robe about her, thrust her feet into her slippers and went out into the hall. There was a thread of light beneath Dr. Baird's door, and without stopping to think, she touched the panels of the door lightly, scarcely more than brushing them for fear a knock would disturb Aunt Susie and Dr. John.

A moment later, the door swung open and Dr. Baird stood there, looking at her, puzzled.

"Yes, Nora? Is it a call?" he asked softly.

"No, I was just anxious to know about the Ferguson baby," she admitted, feeling her face go hot with color.

"The Ferguson baby?" he repeated almost as though he had forgotten there was such a creature. "Oh, yes, of course. Why, he's fine. His mother was terrified because she thought he had a fever and a touch of croup. But we got him comfortable and I think he's going to pull through without any unpleasant after-effects."

"I'm glad," said Nora, and added uncomfortably, "it was only that you had been gone so long and I knew how Mamie had set her heart on the child and I was afraid—after all, it was an emergency."

She thought there was a faint twinkle in Dr. Baird's eyes, and faint as it was, it turned her hot with discomfort.

"Lily and I went back to the dance, and I've just taken her home," he explained. "I was at the Ferguson place less than half an hour."

Looking up at him, her eyes dropped from his face to his collar and there, unmistakably was a small red stain. Lipstick, of course. Lily's lipstick!

She never knew quite what she said or how she got away from him, but the next thing she knew, she was back in her room, with the door closed behind her, and she was trembling. With humiliation, because Dr. Baird had been amused to think she was checking up on him! He wouldn't for a moment believe that she had been merely anxious and concerned about the baby. He would think that she was spying and snooping, that she was jealous!

And suddenly she sank down on the side

of her bed, and her face was as pale as its sun-tan would permit and her eyes were wide and startled. Because she knew that she *was* jealous! Jealous of Dr. Baird and Lily!

She put up her shaking hands and covered her face, there in the darkness, appalled and shocked to the depths of her being by the realization that was sweeping relentlessly over her. She was jealous of Dr. Baird, and you couldn't be jealous unless you were in love with the man! She was, therefore it followed inevitably, in love with Dr. Baird!

"Oh, my goodness!" she gasped inadequately, a breath of sound in the still spring night. "But I can't be. I *won't* be!"

Her mind spoke clearly and coolly to her startled heart: Oh, won't you? You have been from the very first, only you were too stupid to realize it. That's why you could break with Jud and feel nothing but relief. That's why your dislike of Lily has grown into something strong as hatred since you've known that she had her greedy little paws out for Dr. Baird! You can't be in love with him? My good, stupid girl, you *are!*

Only eyes sharpened by jealousy could have detected that tiny, betraying smudge of lipstick on Dr. Baird's collar. Only a heart quivering with love could have been so cruelly hurt by the knowledge that he had been out until this hour with another girl!

No wonder she had been able to talk so calmly, so coolly to Jud about destroying their "understanding" and "starting all over again!" A neat way of extricating herself from Jud so she could concentrate on Dr. Baird! And heck of a lot of good it was going to do her to concentrate on Dr. Baird when the man was quite besotted about Lily!

Nora slid down on the bed and buried her scarlet, burning face against the pillows. But she could not bury the tremulous emotion that shook her body, that centered in her silly heart that cried out for Dr. Baird. Of all the *fools!* To lose her heart to a man, not even knowing she had lost it; and not to discover it until it was too late! Small wonder that, her face smothered in the pillows, she wept until at last in complete exhaustion she fell asleep.

7

THE day set for Dr. John's departure on the eagerly anticipated trip dawned clear and sunny and warm. Dr. John was up at the crack of dawn, and Aunt Susie was in a bustle getting everything ready.

When at last everything had been stowed in the car, Aunt Susie had checked to be sure that he had his money, his traveller's cheques, and all his fishing paraphernalia, he still hesitated, looking from one to the other like an abashed small boy.

"Well, I guess that's it," he said. "Guess I'd better get going."

"If you're planning on going," said Aunt Susie.

Dr. John looked at her swiftly.

"Sure you won't come with me, Susie?" he asked eagerly.

"But you haven't asked me," she protested.

"Well, you know I'd be glad to have you

if you wanted to go," he told her shortly, but would not quite meet her eyes.

"This is a fine time to tell me so," Aunt Susie almost snorted. "When you've been sounding off for weeks about how much you were going to enjoy being alone."

"Well, be kind of nice to have somebody read the road map for me." He was more than ever like an abashed boy, and Nora realized that now that the time for departure had come, he was a little afraid of going alone, and her eyes stung with tears.

"If you wanted company on the trip, you should have said so early enough to give me a chance to get things straightened around so I could leave," Aunt Susie assured him snappishly, but there was a mist in her eyes too.

"Who said I wanted company?" he roared at her so unexpectedly that she jumped. "I suppose you think I'm not to be trusted by myself?"

He strode around to the car, got under the wheel and started the car, while they stood back and watched him. The car rolled down to the highway, turned, and he looked back to raise a hand to them in farewell, before he neatly negotiated a swing around an oncoming truck and speeded up.

Aunt Susie blew her nose vigorously.

"I won't know another peaceful moment until he gets back," she snapped, and strode into the house.

Dr. Baird's eyes followed her, and then he looked down at Nora, who was still looking along the way Dr. John had gone.

"Poor darling," said Nora softly. "He had planned this trip so long, and then when he was ready, he realized he didn't really want to go at all."

"He's a very lucky man," said Dr. Baird quietly. "To have two people like you and Miss Susie to worry about him."

"Well, we've taken care of him and we love him," said Nora simply.

"That was what I meant," said Dr. Baird.

Nora looked up at him, startled by his tone. He was looking down at her gravely, and there was a warmth in his eyes that brought the color to her cheeks.

"It must be a pretty wonderful thing to have somebody care enough about you to worry about you," he said. "I wouldn't know, of course; I grew up in an orphanage and worked my way through school and med. There never seemed to be time to find out about such things as people to worry about you."

"I'm sorry," said Nora huskily.

His smile was as warm as her look had been.

"Thanks," he said quite sincerely. "That's one of the things that drew me to Shellville. It seemed to me that a man might have a much better chance at making friends in a small town."

"And are you glad now that you came?"

"Very glad," said Dr. Baird, and for a moment their eyes held. And then as though her name had been spoken, Nora remembered Lily. Well, of course he was glad he had come to Shellville, for in Shellville he had met Lily! The thought struck at Nora with small, icy-cold claws and she turned away from him swiftly.

"We're all glad, too, Dr. Baird," she told him coolly, above the queer, unaccustomed hurt in her heart. "Not only because it has released Grandfather for his vacation, but because we think you fit into the picture here so well."

Dr. Baird looked down at her, puzzled by the sudden chill in her manner as she walked away toward the office-cottage where a car was already pulling into the parking area and a woman was anxiously helping a child out of it.

"You do think he'll be all right and that he'll enjoy himself, don't you?" Nora burst out suddenly.

Dr. Baird grinned. "Oh, he'll be terribly homesick tonight and won't sleep very much because of it," he assured her. "But by tomorrow, when he gets started on the road, he'll be like a kid let out of school for an unexpected holiday."

"I hope so," said Nora warmly. "Somehow, he looked so forlorn when he went off by himself. Of course, if Aunt Susie had suggested for a moment that she wanted to go with him, he would have lifted the roof in furious protest!"

"I gathered that," admitted Dr. Baird. "They're a wonderful pair. So devoted to each other and so deathly afraid they'll do something to admit it."

Nora said happily, "I'm so relieved you realize that. I was afraid you'd take their bickering and their constant insults to each other seriously."

"I didn't, not even for a moment. I don't see how any one could," said Dr. Baird, as they reached the cottage and she slid the key into the door.

He walked on into the private office, and Nora greeted the waiting patients, and a moment later, Dr. Baird was ready for the first one and the busy day began.

It was shortly before the end of office hours, not quite eleven, when the station-wagon from the Blayde place slid into the parking area and Lily came into the office, lovely and fresh and dainty as always in a simple pale blue chambray dress. Only one patient remained, and Lily noted the fact with satisfaction, as she greeted Nora with her "on parade" manner.

"Hello, Nora, don't you look lovely this morning?" she said sweetly, and added quickly, "but then you always do. Those white uniforms are so becoming, and I love that crazy little cap!"

"Thanks," said Nora, and knew her voice sounded curt. "How is Mr. Blayde this morning?"

Lily grimaced gaily.

"In a perfectly foul humor, which means he's feeling fine," she admitted lightly. "It's only when he's gentle and easily pleased that I worry about him, because then I know he's too sick to want to fight. But he's such a lamb, I can't really ever be angry with him, no matter how he behaves."

Her back was to the patient and her voice was sweet and warm, but to Nora she revealed an expression almost vicious with hatred that gave the ugly lie to her words.

Before Nora could speak, the door opened and Dr. Baird was showing his patient out. He saw Lily and his face lit up with such light that Nora turned sharply away.

"Hi, there," he greeted her. "Don't tell me you're a patient. You're positively blooming with health!"

Lily dimpled demurely and fluttered her extravagant eyelashes at him, as the departing patient lingered a moment to watch and listen, and the one still waiting to be attended to listened with almost visibly distended ears.

"No, of course not. I'm as healthy as a

horse," said Lily gaily. "I was out doing some errands for Uncle Dick, and I was so close I thought I'd run in for a moment instead of calling you."

"Well, I'm mighty glad you did," said Dr. Baird, and Nora told herself that the tone, as well as the look in his eyes, was downright fatuous. "Come on in."

He turned toward his office door and the waiting patient stirred protestingly.

"I've been waitin' for almost an hour, Doc, and I got to get back to work," he protested.

"Oh, I'm sorry," said Dr. Baird, and looked at Lily with humorous dis-appointment.

"I'll run along then," said Lily sweetly. "I just wanted to tell you that I can have the evening off, provided I'm home by midnight."

"Good!" said Dr. Baird happily. "I'll pick you up then, at seven?"

"I'll be waiting," she assured him, and with a gay little wave of her hand to him, and a smile, she was gone.

For a moment Dr. Baird stood smiling, and then he turned briskly to the waiting patient and ushered him into his office.

Nora sat quite still at her desk, her hands clenched tightly, her eyes lowered so that their look could not betray her, even to the sun-drenched empty reception room.

Last night she had faced the fact that she was in love with Dr. Baird; she had also faced the fact that Dr. Baird was in love with Lily. She had thought she faced and accepted those two facts; but seeing Lily and Dr. Baird together, seeing the fatuous look in his eyes as they rested appreciatively on Lily, she knew that she had accepted only the first fact. The second one was going to take some getting used to! A vast deal of getting used to, she repeated to herself.

If Lily was really the girl Dr. Baird thought her, fine and good and sweet, it might not be so hard to know that Dr. Baird was madly in love with her; but Nora would not accept that even from herself. She knew that she would feel just as badly if Dr. Baird had been in love with an earthbound saint! Because with all her heart and soul and mind she wanted Dr. Baird to be in love with *her*. And the very thought was one that should have made her laugh, except that tears were so close she dared not, lest she burst into tears instead.

She tried to center her thoughts on Dr. John, to steady herself. He had looked so lonely and so forlorn, departing on his long-anticipated trip. Perhaps that was the reason for his sudden reluctance, when the moment of departure was on him. He had looked forward to the trip so long that now he was ready to start it, desire for it had gone.

"Ha!" Dr. John had crowed. "That's just what I don't intend to do. I'm not going to let you drag me back here just because somebody stubs his toe, or disputes right of way with a speeding car and loses the decision."

Aunt Susie had stared at him with raised brows.

"Are you trying to tell me that you're going off like this, for an indefinite stay, and that you are not going to leave some sort of address where we can reach you if an emergency crops up?" she demanded, unbelieving.

"That's exactly what I'm telling you," said Dr. John with childlike satisfaction.

"Any emergency Owen can't handle will just have to shift for itself. I'm not coming back until I'm darned good and ready."

"But, John, for heaven's sake, suppose something happens to Nora, or to me? Suppose we *have* to reach you?"

"Owen will be here," Dr. John had insisted, though Nora thought he looked less cocksure and easy in his mind than he wanted to appear.

"All right, then, you blithering idiot," snapped Aunt Susie hotly, "suppose something happens to you?"

"I'll have all sorts of identification on me, the car registration and all that, and if anything happens to me the proper authorities will get in touch with you," Dr. John had told her firmly, but it seemed to Nora there was a brief flicker of uneasiness in his eyes. "Tell you what I'll do; I'll send you a picture postcard every evening when I stop for the night. How'll that do?"

"It won't do at all," Aunt Susie had protested vehemently.

"It'll have to do," Dr. John had insisted. "Matter of fact, I'm not quite sure myself where I'm going. I'm just going to start out and go wherever my

120

fancy takes me. I'll inquire around and find out where the fishing is supposed to be good, and then I'll go there; and if somebody lied to me and the fish aren't biting, then I'll go somewhere else. See how simple it is?"

"Simple is exactly the word I would have used," Aunt Susie had snapped, which had made Dr. John grin like a small boy but had not changed his mind in the least. He had departed in a fine glow at having asserted himself and established a point.

He kept his word about sending them postcards, and after he had been gone a week, there was a brief letter from him saying that he was having a fine time and would be back when he got darned good and ready and not before.

Aunt Susie snorted inelegantly at that but relaxed and went busily about her cherished spring-cleaning. Dr. Baird and Nora settled down to working as a team and all was quiet and peaceful. Except that Nora knew with a sinking heart that Dr. Baird was becoming more and more entranced with Lily; a thought which made her apprehensive for him, as well as for herself. But of course there was nothing she dared do about it, and wisely she did not try.

8

ON Saturday evening, when Dr. John had been gone a week or more, Nora sat on the verandah with Aunt Susie. The nights were much warmer and the wide, old-fashioned verandah was an increasingly pleasant place to sit after dinner. A big canvas swing hung in one corner, shaded from the sun by a big purple clematis vine, now heavy with bloom. There were comfortable, shabby chairs, and Aunt Susie sat in one of these, relaxed and peaceful with the knowledge that she had "a good start" on the cleaning. Nora swung lazily in the big canvas swing, grateful for the peace and quiet.

She tensed slightly as she heard Dr. Baird's footsteps coming swiftly down the stairs, and then he came out to the verandah, looking very well-groomed and, to Nora, very handsome indeed.

"You two look very comfortable," he greeted them, smiling.

Aunt Susie eyed him in the twilight, aided by the yellow light that spilled through the open door from the front hall.

"And you look very handsome and all prettied up for a heavy date," she accused him gaily.

"How very kind you are," laughed Dr. Baird, and gave her a sweeping bow. "I've left a notation on the telephone pad where I can be reached if I'm needed."

"Let's hope we won't have to use it," said Aunt Susie, and added briskly, "have fun."

"Thanks," laughed Dr. Baird. "I'll try to."

A moment later his car went swiftly down the drive and for a little space Nora and Aunt Susie were quiet. Nora's teeth were set hard in her lower lip, her hands clenched tightly. Aunt Susie stared thoughtfully into the gathering dusk.

"What's become of Jud Carter?" demanded Aunt Susie so unexpectedly that Nora jumped.

"Oh, he's around," she said vaguely.

"But not around you," Aunt Susie pointed out. "What happened? Did you quarrel with him?"

"Good heavens, no," Nora snapped, so that it was Aunt Susie's turn to look startled and slightly offended.

"Well, you needn't snap my head off," she protested. "The lad has been here so much that I have thought sometimes of asking why he didn't move his luggage over. And now all of a sudden, not a sign of him. Naturally, I wondered if you had quarrelled."

"Sorry, darling, I didn't mean to snap at you," Nora apologized uncomfortably. "It's just that Jud and I talked things over and decided we'd been mistaken about each other."

Aunt Susie looked at her through the fragile lavender and blue dusk.

"I can't remember a time since you two were in grammar school when you weren't planning some day to get married," she offered at last.

"That was the trouble," Nora said in a small, uneasy rush of words. "We have been going together so long that we've become a habit. We decided it would be wise to stop seeing so much of each other, and sort of play the field and try to make up our minds whether we were really in love, or just so accustomed to each other that we thought we were."

Aunt Susie sighed.

"You young people!" she scorned mildly. "When will you ever learn that being so accustomed to each other is a pretty good basis for a sound and well established marriage?"

"Maybe," admitted Nora, in a tone that said she was not at all convinced. "But it will be several years yet before Jud will be able to support a wife, and in the meanwhile, we thought it would be wise for us to look around."

"I see," commented Aunt Susie dryly. "That's why you haven't had a date since John left, I suppose. Who's doing the looking around—Jud?"

"Oh, well," Nora tried to be off-hand about it, "everybody in Shellville is so accustomed to seeing Jud and me together that it will take a little time for word to get around that I am once more 'available' so that unattached young men will think of asking me for a date."

"Meanwhile, Jud is cavorting around like crazy, I suppose," said Aunt Susie.

"Men have a way of getting word like that around."

Nora leaned forward and spoke earnestly.

"Look, darling, I know you are worried about me, for fear I'll wind up as an old maid. But with my profession, would that be so bad?"

"As an old maid, let me assure you it would be terrible," snapped Aunt Susie. "Oh, don't look sorry for me. I'm perfectly satisfied now. But there was a time when I wanted, more than anything else in the world, a husband, a home and children of my own. But it just didn't work out that way."

"Because you had to look after Grandfather and bring me up," said Nora quietly.

"Oh, I wouldn't say that," protested Aunt Susie halfheartedly. "I've been happy and contented. But I've got sense enough to know that a girl like you, a girl with so much love to give, deserves a better break. More than anything in the world I want to see you married, in your own home and with your own children about you. You'll make a wonderful mother, Nora."

"Thanks, darling," Nora's voice was faintly husky. "But we'd both like for me to be quite sure that it was the husband I wanted, not just somebody I'd known all my life and got accustomed to, and all that. Aunt Susie, there must be something more to it than just that. I've seen girls in love, engaged, getting ready to be married; they were radiant, breathless, wildly excited, and all the rest of it. Being married to Jud wouldn't be like that a bit. Oh, I'm fond of Jud, and we have fun together, but isn't there more to it than that? Than just habit?"

Aunt Susie sat very still for a moment, and though the darkness had thickened so that Nora could no longer see her face, Nora knew that Aunt Susie was looking back down the years toward a decision she had made for the sake of a small, frightened child and a brother devastated by grief.

"Yes, Nora, there's more than that. There's much more than that," she said at last, and her voice was low and not quite even, as she looked out into the soft summer dusk in which a few fireflies were beginning to flash their tiny, moving lights. "There's a glory and a pain. There's the breathless excitement of knowing you are going to see him in a few minutes; there's the rapture of being with him, his hand holding yours. There's the terrible strain of waiting for a telephone that may not ring; of not daring to leave the house for fear he will call while you are gone, and nobody can be trusted to take the message properly. There's walking home from work, going the long way round in the hope of meeting him; looking at every man who comes toward you and not really seeing him because you are looking for just one man. And when you see him, your heart climbs up in your throat and hangs there and there are wings on your feet and you want to run to him and fling yourself into his arms; and at the same time you have a crazy, inexplicable desire to turn and run away from him. Oh, yes, Nora, there's more, much more than just habit."

There were tears in Nora's eyes and her voice was small and husky.

"What happened, Aunt Susie?"

"He died," said Aunt Susie, her tone harsh. And though it must have been many years ago, the ache, the grief, the shock was a frail ghost in her voice, that sounded tired and thin. "Just suddenly, within a few days. A heart attack, the doctors said, but there were complications. Things that, if he had had medical attention when he first realized he was not well, might have spared him for many years. Only he was afraid that if he admitted his illness, the doctors would find an operation and expensive, long-drawn out treatment necessary; we were both saving every penny to speed the day of our marriage."

Her tired voice died, and after a moment she made a slight gesture with her hand.

"He collapsed at his place of business, and was in such pain the doctor had to give him a heavy opiate," she finished evenly. "He never regained consciousness. He never knew me during those three terrible days. I stayed beside his bed, and held him in my arms, and quieted him, but he never knew me."

Nora knelt beside her, holding her

close. And their cheeks were wet with shared tears.

"Poor Aunt Susie," she said unsteadily. "I'm so sorry, darling."

Aunt Susie held her close, and after a moment, she blew her nose vigorously and said sternly, "Now see what you've done. I always did hate a weeping woman!"

She patted Nora fondly and said with an attempt at lightness, "So you see, Nora, there *is* something more than just habit, and with all my heart and soul I hope you'll find it. And if it isn't Jud, then I'm glad you've discovered it in time. I don't want to see you going empty-hearted all your life. You see, I had John and you to fill my heart, but we're all you've got. You'll be so terribly alone when we are gone, unless you find your love!"

Nora clung to her for a moment, her face hidden against her aunt's bony shoulder. Fighting against the almost unbearable temptation to reveal her heart; to admit that she had found her love, but that he had found someone else! But of course she mustn't say that; she mustn't let Aunt Susie know that she loved Dr. Baird and that Dr. Baird was mad about

Lily! It was a grief and a heartache she must bear alone, and not share with this loving, devoted heart that would grieve with and for her.

"Thank you for telling me, darling," she said huskily at last.

Aunt Susie answered with almost her accustomed tartness, "Well, after all, I didn't want you to run around thinking no man had ever found me attractive. Even an old woman like me has some pride!"

She was trying so hard to lighten the moment's tension that Nora exerted herself to help. But long after they had said good-night and Nora was in bed, she lay wide awake staring into the darkness, thinking back over the brief story Aunt Susie had told her.

For a moment she saw herself in Aunt Susie's place: standing beside Dr. Baird's bed-side, knowing that he loved her as she loved him, but that now, beneath the merciful opiate, he was as lost to her as he could be after Death had closed about him. And she hid her face against her pillow and wept for all the lonely, heart-empty women in the world like Aunt Susie. And she wondered, in brief panic

132

that she fought with all her strength, if she, too, might join that lonely sisterhood. Because she would not love again; that she knew with a clarity that was startling.

9

THE days slid by, with spring giving way to summer, and with Nora and Dr. Baird working together smoothly and efficiently as any doctor dreams the ideal nurse will work with him. Dr. Baird was obviously as much absorbed in Lily as before, but of course never mentioned her name to Nora.

Nora was awakened close to midnight by the shrilling of the telephone on the table beside her. Sleepily, she took the receiver off the hook, instantly wide awake and alert as a man's frightened, babbling voice spoke in her ear.

"You got to come quick, Miss Nora, you and the Doc. Mary's took bad. Her Maw says she may lose the young'un. Hurry, Miss Nora, hurry!"

"Be right with you, Lem," said Nora, and clicked the receiver in place.

She caught up her robe, thrust her feet into her slippers and ran down the hall to

Dr. Baird's door, rapping sharply on it. She heard his answering voice.

"Martha Turner," said Nora swiftly. "We were afraid of trouble there, remember? Her husband just called."

"Be right with you," said Dr. Baird.

"Right," said Nora, and ran back to her room.

There was no question but that she would go with him. They had been uneasy about this patient. Martha Turner, sixteen, yet already married and pregnant. A frail, not overly bright girl, stubborn, refusing to take care of herself during her pregnancy as she had been ordered by Dr. Baird; a girl who lived in Slabtown, out beyond Shellville in an isolated section of "poor whites" where wives were expected to be strong as mules, and to assume the heaviest of tasks.

Donning her uniform, catching up the scrap of a cap, adjusting it as she went, Nora ran out of her room just as Dr. Baird emerged from his, and without a word they hurried down the steps and out to his car, parked as always where he could make the fastest start on any emergency case.

As he drove, with Nora directing him to

the narrow, bumpy dirt road that led to the isolated settlement, they discussed the case, each admitting uneasiness for the girl and for the expected baby.

Slabtown had grown up about an abandoned lumber camp. One by one, families of poor whites, subsisting on patchy little vegetable gardens, on fishing and hunting, had taken possession of the shacks built by the lumber company to house its transient workers. A drearier, more depressing place for the residence of human beings it would be hard to find, thought Nora as the car jounced complainingly over the corduroy road, built for trucks and log-rollers, and the lights picked out the dingy clutter of shacks.

As Dr. Baird brought the car to a halt, a man ran stumbling towards them, and Nora caught the sour scent of whiskey and knew the man was more than half-drunk on the foul "swamp-water" moonshine these people were accused of making and selling, though the revenue officers had never been able to get enough evidence against any of them for an arrest.

"Doc, you got to fix things," he stammered wildly. "She's took bad. And just this afternoon she was fine. Why, she hoed out the garden," he babbled.

Dr. Baird swore at him, even as he jumped out of the car and followed Nora swiftly to the lighted cabin.

A bent old woman, toothless, frowsy, stood in the doorway, and as the frantic husband came stumbling along the path, she crowed viciously, "I tole him he ain't no right to whup her, the shape she's in."

Nora caught her breath in shocked horror, and Dr. Baird thrust the old woman unceremoniously aside, and went swiftly to the ancient bedstead where the girl lay in a tumble of soiled bed linen.

One look told Nora that the girl was in the narrow borderline between life and death, but she and Dr. Baird went swiftly, efficiently to work, with Nora anticipating Dr. Baird's needs before he spoke.

It was a bitter, heart-breaking business, but as moments became hours, Nora and Dr. Baird knew they were winning the grim battle. And when at last the thin, angry cry of the new-born baby made itself heard, they straightened for just a moment and grinned at each other triumphantly. They had won. The girl would live and, barring unforeseen complications, so would the baby.

Dr. Baird gave stern orders to the old midwife and to the young mother's white-faced parents, before he and Nora stepped out into the cool, crisp darkness of the hour before dawn.

"How is she, Doc?" babbled the husband.

"She'll live, and so will the baby," said Dr. Baird sternly. "I'm filing charges against you at the sheriff's office, for beating her, though. You ought to be shot."

The man stepped back as from a blow, and in the thin yellow light from the cabin door, his unshaven, gaunt face took on an ugly look.

"Reckon you'll have to git somebody to swear I laid a finger on her, Doc," he growled. "And you ain't gonna get nobody to do that, 'cause I didn't."

Dr. Baird turned to the cabin and addressed the old midwife.

"You'll swear to the complaint, won't you?" he demanded.

The old woman shot a furtive glance

toward the husband's threatening face, and then looked up innocently at Dr. Baird.

"I don't reckon I know of any complaint, Doc," she said smoothly.

"You told me as I came in a while ago that you tried to keep Lem from whipping his wife," said Dr. Baird sharply.

"Why, Doc, I reckon sure you musta been mistaken," said the old woman gently. "I'm sich a liar you cain't hardly believe more'n half o' whut I say. But I don't recollect sayin' anythin' like that."

Nora saw the helpless anger that blazed in Dr. Baird's face as he turned to look at Lem Turner, who was watching him narrowly.

"I ain't gonna hold it against you, Doc, that you thought anything like that about me," said Lem, derision in his eyes. "I'm mighty obliged you saved my wife and the young-'un. It's a boy, ain't it?"

"It's a girl," said Dr. Baird, and added deliberately, "poor little devil!"

Lem made a gesture with a big, gnarled hand.

"Oh, well, gal-young-'uns ain't so bad," he said forgivingly. "Reckon wimmen is useful same as men, even if they cain't plow as good."

Dr. Baird smothered whatever furious retort might have trembled on his tongue and guided Nora to the car. She said nothing as he backed the car, turned and drove back toward the highway. But at last as they were driving back toward town she smiled faintly.

"I know how you feel, Doctor," she said quietly. "But it's no use trying to get anything down in Slabtown to change the people. They're a queer breed. They fight furiously among themselves but put up a solid front against any outsider who comes in and tries to take a hand."

"Sure, I know," he agreed unhappily. "I've seen it in charity wards. Some poor devil of a woman is brought into Emergency, beaten black and blue and swears to high heaven that she fell. Even when you know she has been mercilessly beaten by some brute of a drunken husband. I used to hear torch-singers wailing away about 'My Man' and boasting that he beat her and kicked her, but she still loved him because he was hers. I had a contemptuous scorn for such foolishness, until I interned

140

at Mercy Hospital in Atlanta, and saw some of them. Not singing 'torch songs' but lying their bruised and battered heads off to protect the men they loved! How in blazes *can* a woman go on loving that sort of brute?"

Nora said dryly, "Women are funny people."

"And the sensible thing for a man is not to try to understand them," Dr. Baird agreed grimly.

Ahead of them, lights blazed, marking an all-night diner.

"What about coffee?" he suggested.

"I can't think of anything at the moment I'd like more," said Nora frankly. "I'm famished."

"Good!" Dr. Baird swept the car from the highway and into the large parking area in front of the diner, brilliantly lit, lonely out here in the woods. "These places usually have pretty good coffee, and maybe they'll be able to do something about bacon and eggs."

He parked the car, and Nora got out and walked ahead of him to the diner. As she opened the door, there was a swift rustle, a gasp, and for a moment Nora looked full into the startled, white face of Lily Halstead. The next moment, with a flicker of pink linen skirts, Lily had raced to the small, narrow door at the back of the diner, beneath the word "Ladies" and the door shut behind her.

Nora stood rock-still for a moment, all but holding her breath. Had Dr. Baird seen her? She looked swiftly at the table from which Lily had fled. A man sat there, watching her with amused, derisive eyes. A man with a narrow, ferrety sort of face, clean-shaven, dressed in cheap, flashy clothes, who watched her appraisingly through the smoke of his cigarette.

Nora turned as Dr. Baird came up behind her, and let go of her held breath. For he had gone back to the car to get his instrument bag, and he was saying briskly, "Sorry I held you up. Thought I'd better not leave it in the car and tempt some thief to swipe it."

He was smiling at her, holding the door open for her, and Nora knew that he had not seen Lily. She drew a deep breath, walked to a table that faced the Ladies' Room and sat down, her back to Lily's companion, facing the door where Lily hid.

She was trembling slightly but she managed to conceal it, while Dr. Baird paused at the counter to give their order and then joined her, holding out a package of cigarettes.

Nora's hand shook slightly in spite of her efforts at control as she accepted the cigarette and leaned toward the lighted match Dr. Baird held for her.

"Tired?" he asked, smiling, misunderstanding her trembling. "It's been quite a session, after all."

"Quite," she agreed, relieved that he could accept that explanation for her nervousness.

She was sharply conscious of the man behind her, knowing that he could hear every word they spoke, and she felt that she could see his acrid amusement in the situation. It meant nothing to him, of course, except that it amused him. Lily had been white-faced with panic, before she fled. That, naturally, Nora could understand. After all, no respectable girl would be caught in such a place as this at a little before four in the morning. Not unless she had an excellent excuse, as she herself did. Still in uniform, and accompanied by Dr. Baird, she need have no fear of her presence here being misunderstood. But for Lily, there was no such alibi.

She wondered about Lily's companion. He looked cheap and flashy and dangerous. Knowing Lily as she did, Nora felt quite sure that there was an ugly significance to their being here together.

She was grateful for Dr. Baird's casual conversation and exerted herself to keep up with her share of it, until the surly counterman placed platters of food and cups of strong, hot coffee before them. But the appetite of which she had boasted was gone, and she picked at the food, her eyes slipping now and then beyond Dr. Baird to the door behind which Lily hovered.

"I thought you were hungry?" asked Dr. Baird, puzzled when she seemed not to be interested in her food. "Is something wrong with it?"

"Oh, no, of course not," said Nora hastily. "I guess I'm just too tired to enjoy food. The coffee is wonderful."

"You'd better keep up your strength,

my girl," he chided her lightly. "There'll be time for only an hour or two of sleep before the daily grind begins. Or had you thought of that?"

"Oh, I'm used to this sort of thing," Nora assured him with a false gaiety. "Grandfather says there is an unwritten law against any baby being born in the daytime, especially when its parents live in some hard-to-reach spot like Slabtown. Only he insists that it's usually the one night of the year when we have a blizzard that most of them elect to come into the world."

"It's a thought many country doctors share with him, I can assure you." Dr. Baird grinned and launched into an amusing anecdote that carried them through the rest of the meal.

Once, while they finished a second cup of coffee and a second cigarette, the door of the Ladies' Room inched open just enough for Nora to see Lily peering out, angry and baffled that they continued so long.

"More coffee?" suggested Dr. Baird at last.

"Not another drop, thanks," said Nora, and rose with relief.

Dr. Baird paid the check, and as Nora passed the table where Lily's companion still sat, Nora's eyes were drawn to him irresistibly. The man looked her over so deliberately, so slowly that she felt the color burn hotly in her cheeks and her head went up. But she went out of the door Dr. Baird held open for her and down to the car without betraying herself.

When they were back in the car and headed once more towards town, Dr. Baird drove negligently, his thoughts obviously busy.

"You know, Nora," he said quietly, "this thing called love is a darned funny business, isn't it?"

Startled, Nora looked swiftly up at him.

"Is it?" was the best she could manage by way of an answer.

"Of course, I don't suppose I really have the right to speak authoritatively about such a subject," he admitted with an oddly boyish grin. "Oh, I've imagined myself in love several times, but nothing ever came of it, so I know it was just a false alarm. But somehow, I can't imagine ever loving someone you can't respect or trust. Yet these women like the Turner girl who go on sticking with brutes like her husband —what makes 'em tick, I wonder?"

Nora managed a small and not very convincing laugh.

"I'm afraid I wouldn't know, either," she admitted, "never having been in love myself."

He looked down at her swiftly.

"But aren't you engaged to young Carter?" he demanded in surprise.

"Not any more," Nora said swiftly. "We found out it was—well, what you called a false alarm, so we called it off."

"I'm sorry," said Dr. Baird.

"Why?"

He looked at her, his eyebrows raised, smiling slightly.

"You're quite right, it's none of my business, is it?" he offered tacit apology. "I just meant that he seemed such a nice guy and you both seemed very much in love."

"We were not," Nora told him quietly. "We have known each other all our lives, and we sort of drifted into being engaged. A habit, I think it was. And then one day we realized that it wasn't the real thing. It's quite simple."

"You make it sound so," he admitted. "And thanks for telling me."

"There's no secret about it," Nora pointed out. "We are each free to date others, to look around us and see what's going on."

"And then if you do find out later on that it wasn't just habit, you can pick up where you left off," said Dr. Baird. "That's very wise."

Nora all but laughed in his face. As if she hadn't already found out that what she had felt for Jud was a very dim and frail thing compared to what she felt for *him!* As if she could ever "pick up where she had left off" with Jud, now that she knew there was a glory of love that made her affection for Jud merely a damp spark!

He had said, "I can't imagine ever loving someone you can't respect and trust." And yet he was in love with Lily Halstead, and Lily was a thorough no-good and not fit to touch his shoe-laces! Only she couldn't ever tell him, and Lily would see to it that he never found out! When she said good-night to Dr. Baird and went on to her room for a brief rest before resuming her job, there were tears falling in her heart. Tears for the dear dream of loving him, and tears of pity for the bitter disillusionment he must inevitably know some day, if he went on loving Lily, the faithless.

10

SHE was at work at her desk in the office the next morning shortly after Dr. Baird had departed on his morning calls, when the station-wagon swung sharply into the parking area out front, and Lily came in.

For a moment the two girls eyed each other, the sword of bitter enmity sharp and clean-cut between them. Lily looked lovely and flower-like as always in a crisp pink and white checked gingham dress, a matching ribbon tied through her shining hair. But her face was set and cold and her eyes held a vicious glint.

"Well?" she demanded when Nora showed no disposition to break the silence between them. "Did you tell him?"

"About seeing you at the place with that horrible little man? No, of course not," said Nora curtly.

Lily relaxed and the vicious glint in her eyes was replaced by relief.

"I should have known you wouldn't,"

she said maliciously. "You're so pure and noble, aren't you, darling?"

"I'm not a tattle-tale, and anyway, you and I both know that if I *had* told him, and he had dragged you out of your hiding-place, you would have had some very plausible excuse, though I have to admit that I can't help wondering what your excuse could have been."

Lily laughed. That lovely, soft laugh that to masculine ears sounded like the chiming of delicate silver bells, though it rang very differently on feminine ears.

"Oh, I had that all figured out," she drawled. "I would have told him that I had come out looking for him, and because I was afraid to drive in the country alone that late at night, Eddie had come with me."

Nora eyed her with unconcealed bitterness.

"And of course you have already planned the sort of emergency that would make it necessary for you to drive all over the country looking for Dr. Baird," she said grimly.

Lily laughed, raising her eyebrows lightly.

"Well, of course," she said sweetly. "Poor dear Uncle Dick would have had a 'bad spell,' or else maybe Mother. Oh, I'd have thought of something."

"I'm sure you would."

Lily studied her for a moment, her lovely head tilted.

"You know, Nora, you amaze me," she said in an unwonted burst of honesty. "Any other woman in the world would have been tickled silly to tell on me. But not you! And yet I have the craziest feeling that you're in love with darling Owen yourself."

"That's ridiculous!" snapped Nora, her face hot.

"Ridiculous for you to love him? Of course, darling, because he's in love with me," said Lily sweetly, preening herself. "And no man I want ever gets away from me, darling. Especially not to a meek, mousy little gal like you!"

"I amaze you?"

Lily laughed again.

"Oh, sure, a girl like you could never hope to understand a girl like me," she admitted shamelessly. "I'm smart! I fight for what I want, and I use any weapons I can get my hands on. I'd have told on you in a minute last night, if I'd been in your place. But then, I won't ever be in your place 'cause I'm too smart."

"Get out," said Nora savagely.

"Of course, sweetie." Lily was completely undisturbed by Nora's anger. In fact, she seemed to relish it. "There's nothing to make me want to linger, when Owen isn't here. Be seein' you."

As she turned to go, Nora asked quietly, "How is Jud?"

Lily paused and turned, her eyebrows going up.

"Oh, you know about Jud and me, do you?" she said lightly. "I was wondering if you did. You don't have much luck with your men, do you, darling?"

"I'm not sure that what you have could exactly be called luck," Nora pointed out shortly. "After all, you can't very easily marry both of them, can you? Not at the same time anyway."

Lily gasped in honest astonishment.

"Marry?" she repeated as though she had never heard the word in her life. "You surely don't think I'm fool enough to *marry* either of them, do you?"

Nora blinked.

"I admit I was a little puzzled," she said dryly.

"I wouldn't marry any man on earth, unless he was worth millions and millions. If he was, I'd marry him if he looked like Gargantua and behaved like Jack the Ripper," said Lily grimly. "But marry a two-bit shyster like Jud? Or a saw-bones like Owen? Nora, darling, be yourself. I'm only having fun with them!"

"That, of course, I had guessed."

"Of course you had, angel. The important thing is that *they* haven't!" Lily purred her satisfaction. "All I want from Jud is the dope on Uncle Dick's will; then you can have him back."

"You'll never get the 'dope,' as you call it, on Mr. Blayde's will from Jud!"

"Want to bet?"

For a moment the two eyed each other, and then Nora clenched her fists and turned away from the lovely, malicious creature at the door.

"I'm wondering," she said thinly at last, "what you want from Owen."

Lily laughed lightly.

"Not a thing," she said coolly, deliberately. "Except to take him away from you.'

Nora turned sharply beneath the impact of that, her eyes wide and startled.

"But, Lily, that's crazy. You can't take him away from me, because you can't take something some one never had! Dr. Baird scarcely knows I am alive, except as a nurse who works with him," she stammered.

Lily looked her over from the crisp, impertinent little white cap to the tips of her sensible, foot-saving white oxfords, and once more laughed that tinkling little laugh that made Nora's nerves tense with dislike.

"Oh, but if he had seen you first, before he saw me, he might very easily have fallen in love with you," she drawled. "And I'm smart enough to know that a gal like me has her work cut out for her when she tries to take a man away from a gal like you *after* he's hooked. It was just my usual good luck that I happened along that first morning he came, so that I could get in my 'licks' before he got to know you better! And now, he's right *here!*"

She held out her hand, palm upward,

and curled her fingers above the palm, smiling, triumphant, malicious.

Nora knew, with a tightening of her body, that Lily spoke the truth. Dr. Baird was in the palm of her hand, hers to do with as she liked, and the thought was an almost unendurable bitterness.

"And what about the man you were with this morning?" she asked quietly at last above the pain and the desolation that shook her.

"Eddie?" Lily's eyes softened and some of the malice went out of them. "Oh, he's just a friend of mine; a very good friend. Strictly for laughs. We have fun together; he's *my* kind of man! Takes what he wants, where he finds it and the heck with whoever it might have belonged to first."

She was thoughtful for a moment, and then she lifted her shoulders in a shrug of dismissal.

"Eddie's on his way up," she said at last. "But he doesn't want to be hampered by a wife; even a wife like me, who could be such a tremendous help to him. I could be, but he won't believe it. He's after really big money and no strings to tie him down. So—" She lifted a hand, palm upward, in a little gesture as though she tossed something away, "we play around and have fun and neither of us takes it seriously for so much as a bare-faced moment."

Nora said huskily, "You really *are* rotten, aren't you?"

"I suppose so, from your viewpoint," said Lily coolly. "But I'd much rather be me, rotten as I am, than you, stuck here in this nasty little town for the rest of your life, looking after the sick and injured. You can be Florence Nightingale, I want to be somebody important with a lot of money and lovely clothes and jewels and places to go every night."

There was nothing Nora could say, nothing that would have had any effect, and Lily grinned at her impishly.

"I get a big kick out of you, Nora," she said sweetly. "I know I can let my hair down and be really myself with you and nobody will ever know, because you'll never tattle. You aren't the tattling kind. Besides, who'd believe you if you did?"

"The women would," Nora pointed out dryly.

"Oh, *women!*" Lily's disgust and

contempt was in her voice and in the small, vulgar gesture of dismissal she made as she laughed and walked out of the office.

Nora sat very still watching her through the window as she walked, slim and lovely and radiantly sure of herself, to the station-wagon. Of course all that Lily had said was true. No man would believe another woman's tale-bearing against her, even if a woman could so lower all her standards as to carry talks on her. Lily was a disease that ran rampant, unchecked, because so far nobody had been able to dream up a cure for women like her!

11

WHEN Dr. Baird came back for his afternoon office hours, Nora had herself well in hand, and stood beside his desk, putting down a file of papers that had come in the morning mail.

"The X-rays, Dr. Baird, and the report on Clarissa Blaisdell," she told him. "She and her mother have the first appointment of the afternoon. They are due in fifteen minutes." Dr. Baird frowned down at the papers as he studied them swiftly.

"Confirming our diagnosis that there is nothing organically wrong?" he murmured thoughtfully, and looked up at her, smiling slightly. "So we were right, eh?"

Nora flushed as she smiled at him.

"It was your diagnosis, Dr. Baird," she told him demurely, loving this moment in which they were close and aligned solidly against the world.

"It was ours, because as a woman you

guessed what was chiefly wrong," he pointed out.

"Well, of course I don't know the Blaisdells at all," admitted Nora frankly. "They came to Shellville only a few years ago and have a lot of money and move in a much more rarified atmosphere than I do. But Mrs. Blaisdell is such a dominerring type, and Clarissa looks as if she'd never been allowed a thought of her own since the day she was born."

"She is being slowly but surely smothered to death," said Dr. Baird grimly. "Managed and dominated and generally 'sat upon' until she's as helpless as a baby. That can be murder just as surely as if a pistol or a knife had been used; it's as deadly and far more cruel. Yet the law is unable to touch the criminal responsible."

Nora drew a deep breath and nodded in agreement. Yet when at three o'clock an expensive sedan swept haughtily into the parking area, Nora braced herself to greet the Blaisdells as courteously as any other patients who came to the office, hiding her dislike of the woman who came striding into the office as though she owned the place and didn't think much of it.

She was a big woman, smartly dressed in an expensively simple shantung frock of pale gray, with touches of delft-blue that were the color of her slightly protruding but undeniably fine eyes. Her hair was fashionably "blued" and elaborately curled and waved and "set." There was a simple strand of pearls hugging the high neck-line of her shantung frock, and matching pearls in her ears.

The girl who moved slowly behind her looked, Nora told herself, like a frightened rabbit. Whatever claims to beauty she may once have had were wiped out by her pallor, by the terror barely concealed in her eyes, and by her shrinking, uneasy manner. Her dress, as expensive and well-cut as her mother's, was of a peculiarly unbecoming shade of marigold yellow. Worn by a girl with more color, of a more positive personality, it might have been quite becoming and striking; but it wiped out what faint shreds of looks Clarissa Blaisdell might once have had.

"Good afternoon, nurse." Mrs Blaisdell's manner was that of royalty being gracious to an underling of such small importance it was absurd to try to remember the name. "I have an appointment with the doctor. I'm Mrs. Blaisdell."

"Dr. Baird is waiting, Mrs. Blaisdell," said Nora politely. And while Mrs. Blaisdell did not quite say "Naturally!" her manner implied it.

She swept past Nora, her head high, and Clarissa crept after her, giving Nora a shy, frightened ghost of a smile.

"Will you come in, too, please, Nora?" called Dr. Baird, and Nora, armed with a note-book and pencil, seated herself beside the desk, ready for whatever service he might require of her.

"Well, Doctor?" Mrs. Blaisdell began curtly.

"I've received the reports on the blood-tests and the X-rays and the general check-up made on your daughter, Mrs. Blaisdell," said Dr. Baird quietly. "I'm very happy to report that there is nothing wrong organically."

Mrs. Blaisdell turned on Clarissa, who was perched on the edge of her chair, and who recoiled from her mother's swift movement so that once more Nora was reminded of a frightened rabbit.

"There!" snapped Mrs. Blaisdell sharply. "You see? I knew all along that there was nothing wrong with you. That you were just pretending and malingering. I'm disgusted with you."

She turned to Dr. Baird and rose.

"Thank you, Doctor," she said graciously. "You've confirmed what I believed all along: that she was simply moping and trying to gain sympathy for herself. She has always been a bitter disappointment to me."

Dr. Baird's face was cold and set.

"Sit down, Mrs. Blaisdell," he said in a tone that made the woman blink, though she obeyed him. "If I had told you your daughter was suffering from a terrible disease, an incurable malady, I wonder how you would have reacted."

Puzzled, offended, Mrs. Blaisdell said haughtily, "I would have been shocked and alarmed, of course. But you say there is nothing wrong."

"I said nothing organically wrong," stated Dr. Baird grimly. "The truth is that your daughter is very ill, in her mind and in her spirit."

Mrs. Blaisdell gasped, and beneath her carefully applied make-up, she paled, as she glanced at her pallid, big-eyed daughter.

"You mean mentally ill?" she gasped as though it were with difficulty she got the words out.

"I mean your daughter is starved for love, for honest affection and tenderness," began Dr. Baird.

Anger flamed in Mrs. Blaisdell's eyes.

"Are you trying to say that I do not love my daughter?"

"That's exactly what I'm saying."

"That is ridiculous, insulting and absurd," she cried hotly. "I have devoted myself to her since the day she was born. I've scarcely had a thought that was not for her. She has been shielded and protected and provided for. She has had everything in the world that money could buy."

"Except the one thing that every living creature needs, which is love," Dr. Baird said quietly, making no effort to disguise the contempt in his voice. "Mrs. Blaisdell, tiny new-born babies know the need for love. Many, many experiments, careful study, have proven that a baby's need for love begins with birth and lasts as long as it lives."

Mrs. Blaisdell had herself under control now, but the look in her eyes was ugly.

"Really, Doctor, I did not know that you were a psychiatrist," she sneered.

"All doctors are, to a certain extent, Mrs. Blaisdell, because healing the body is not possible unless the mind is healed, too. People have to *want* to live before a doctor can restore them to health. Your daughter is sick, Mrs. Blaisdell, because never in her life has she known an honest, unquestioning love."

So unexpectedly that they all turned to her startled, Clarissa spoke.

"That's not quite true, Dr. Baird," she said huskily. "My father loved me, even though I was a plain and unattractive baby and a plain, awkward child. He loved me very dearly. But he died when I was nine."

Dr. Baird's eyes were warm, sympathetic.

"I'm sorry," he said gently. "Was he ill long?"

165

Clarissa lifted her chin and her eyes looked straight into her mother's with a bitterness that made Nora draw an inaudible breath.

"He shot himself," Clarissa said clearly, almost accusingly.

"An accident, of course," Mrs. Blaisdell said hurriedly, and her eyes were bitter on her daughter.

"It was not an accident," Clarissa said evenly. "He couldn't bear living any longer, under Mother's torture."

"Clarissa, you horrible girl, how dare you say such a thing?" cried Mrs. Blaisdell furiously.

"Because it's true," said Clarissa still in that quiet, even tone. "It's always been your money, Mother. Dad was so madly in love with you that he was blind to the danger of being mistaken for a fortune hunter. He loved you so much and he was so sure of your love for him that he thought together you could lick the gossip and the unpleasantness. You could have, too, if you'd loved him enough to live with him *his* way and let him support you and me."

Mrs. Blaisdell seemed to have forgotten

Dr. Baird and Nora, and to feel that she and the girl were alone here in this small room. Nora could see in the woman's white, shocked face how dazed she was at her daughter's devastating frankness. Probably, Nora reflected, it was the first time in her life Clarissa had ever dared speak out against her mother.

"I suppose you think I should have thrown away the fortune my father left me, and have gone to live in a pigsty on your father's miserable earnings," she flashed.

"If you had loved him enough——" began Clarissa relentlessly.

"I've had just about enough of this nonsense about 'love,'" snapped Mrs. Blaisdell furiously. "It's a silly, meaningless word that only a fool takes as important. Your father and I had a good life, and his death was an accident."

Once more she stood up, and now she was sharply conscious of Nora and Dr. Baird, and turned the fury of her bitter gaze on them.

"I hope you are satisfied with the scene your absurd attitude has brought about," she told him hotly. "You may be quite sure that I shall see to it none of my friends come near you. I was a fool to come here, but I had heard that you were quite good and I was deeply concerned for my daughter's health."

"But now that you have learned the truth about her illness, you intend to do nothing about it," said Dr. Baird mildly, and his tone made it a statement, not a question.

"I shall do whatever I think best," snapped Mrs. Blaisdell, and turned to the door. "Come, Clarissa."

The girl's voice was so quiet that for an instant her mother seemed not to have heard it, and her hand was already on the door before she whirled to look with unbelieving eyes into Clarissa's eyes.

"No, Mother," Clarissa said again as though to make sure that her mother had really heard. "I'm not coming."

"You're not coming? What nonsense is this?"

"I'm never coming home again. Not to that place you call home," stated Clarissa. "I'm going to find a job, and a life of my own."

"Why, you silly fool!" raged Mrs. Blaisdell viciously. "What could *you* do to earn a living? You never turned your hand to an honest day's work in your life. You've never been trained for anything."

"And for that, Mrs. Blaisdell, you should do penance," said Dr. Baird grimly.

"You keep out of this," snapped Mrs. Blaisdell hotly. "All this is your fault."

"I'm proud to admit it," said Dr. Baird, and gave Clarissa a warm, encouraging smile. "I think your daughter is going to be all right, from here on out."

"All right?" Mrs. Blaisdell's tone could not have expressed greater anger, more helpless bitterness. "Of course she doesn't mean a word of it. I can't think what has come over her."

"I can't, either," admitted Clarissa unexpectedly. "I just know that for the first time since Dad died, I feel alive. As if there might be some happiness for me in the future. As if I could breathe again! And it's wonderful."

She looked at Dr. Baird with shining eyes.

"I don't know how to thank you," she said unsteadily.

"By being happy and making a good life for yourself," said Dr. Baird, smiling.

"A good life? By starving to death? I refuse to give her one penny, until she comes home and behaves herself," snapped Mrs. Blaisdell sharply. "We'll see how good a life she can have. Earning her own living! How, may I ask?"

"I've got that little income Dad left me," began Clarissa, and Nora saw that for a moment there was a touch of the old panic in her eyes.

"Less than a hundred dollars a month!" sneered Mrs. Blaisdell. "You spend that much on nylons."

"I don't," Clarissa corrected her. "You may. I don't know. Because I have never in my life gone shopping for myself or selected anything that I was to wear."

"Well, can I help it if your taste is so undependable? Believe me, as the one who pays the bills, I can assure you that ninety-six dollars a month would not pay for one outfit that I choose for you."

"Maybe if I choose them myself, they needn't cost so much," said Clarissa, undisturbed, and looked down with frank distaste at the expensive, unbecoming frock she wore. "I can't remember when I have ever had a frock I really liked, or felt comfortable in."

Mrs. Blaisdell was watching her with a curious startled look, almost as though she saw her for the first time. And now for the first time there was a warmth, perhaps born of the new uncertainty in her heart, as she glanced uneasily at Dr. Baird and Nora, who were watching Clarissa.

"I think we have provided sufficient amusement for Dr. Baird and this young woman," she said then. "Come along, Clarissa; we can talk this over in privacy."

"There's nothing to talk over, Mother," said Clarissa quietly. "My mind is made up. And for the first time in my life, I'm not afraid of you."

Nora heard Dr. Baird mumur just above his breath, "Good girl!"

Mrs. Blaisdell's eyes widened and for a moment she was speechless.

"Afraid of me?" she gasped. "Clarissa, how can you say that? Why, I never punished you in my life; I never even spanked you when you were little."

Clarissa shrugged.

"Oh, physical punishment isn't

important, Mother," she said gently. "I don't think I would have minded if you had beaten me black and blue, if you had then taken me in your arms and told me you loved me. I always knew that you were disappointed in me. You always reminded me you and Dad had wanted a son; and you always told me how plain and unattractive I was. I used to dream about a day when you'd turn to me suddenly and say, 'Why, darling, how pretty you are.' But you never did. Oh, I know you couldn't have said it in truth, because I have never been pretty and I never will be."

"You're wrong there, Clarissa," Dr. Baird interrupted so unexpectedly that Clarissa turned startled eyes on him almost as though she had forgotten his presence. "Potentially, you are a very beautiful woman. Your hair, your eyes, the shape of your face; you have a very fine bone structure. You tell her, Nora, by what steps she can reveal her real beauty."

Nora smiled warmly at Clarissa.

"I'll be glad to, Clarissa, any time you like," she offered.

"You're filling her up with a lot of

moonshiny nonsense," protested Mrs. Blaisdell self-righteously. "It's much better for her to know the truth and face it than to build her up with silly, false hopes."

"Like your telling me ever since I was sixteen that no man would ever fall in love with me for myself, but that any man who came wooing me would really have his eye on the fact that I am your heiress?" said Clarissa quietly.

Dr. Baird said sharply, "Surely, Mrs. Blaisdell, you wouldn't teach her that?"

Mrs. Blaisdell turned on him in fury.

"And why not? Do you think I wanted to see her make the same mistake I did, for lack of being properly trained?"

Dr. Baird stared at her for a long moment, and then he drew a deep breath and shook his head as though to clear it of a fog of unpleasant thoughts.

"If you had crippled your daughter physically, there would be laws to protect her," he said at last. "But for what you have done to her, and it is a thousand times worse, there is no defense. But I think your punishment may be, some day, to realize what a hideous thing you have done and to suffer for it."

"Dr. Baird, I don't know by what authority you have taken it on yourself to insult me and to make such accusations," Mrs. Blaisdell was trembling with outrage. "But I shan't forget it, I assure you."

"I'm sure you won't, and I'm glad for that," said Dr. Baird grimly.

"I won't forget, either, Dr. Baird," said Clarissa, and she was radiant. "I don't quite know what happened to me. I have always been so afraid of Mother."

"Clarissa!" gasped her mother, shocked and affronted.

"Be quiet, Mother," said Clarissa without even looking at her. "But somehow, now I don't feel a bit afraid of her. I can hold my own with her now, and I shall be grateful to you as long as I live."

"Good!" said Dr. Baird, smiling warmly as he took the hand she extended to him and held it closely. "Your mother wants only the best for you, Clarissa, always. The reason she has always dominated you so sternly is that she has been convinced that only she knew what was best for you. She has never learned that human beings learn by making mistakes; that a baby learns to walk only by stumbling, falling and picking itself up again, and that constantly shielding and helping him or her is the most unkind thing anyone can ever do."

Nora caught the startled, puzzled look Mrs. Blaisdell gave Dr. Baird, as though surprised that he could understand her so well.

"Will you come to dinner, Dr. Baird? And you, too, please?" Clarissa's warm look included Nora shyly. "Remember, you promised you'd help me make myself more attractive."

"It will be fun, and easy," Nora assured her sincerely.

For a moment Clarissa's eyes clung to Nora, and then she said impulsively, "I've never had a friend. I think you would be a wonderful friend."

"That's a wonderful compliment; thank you very much," Nora replied.

Clarissa beamed at them both and turned toward the door.

"Come along, Mother," she said lightly. And, blinking, Mrs. Blaisdell followed her to the door, perhaps the only time in her life she had ever followed anybody.

At the door Mrs. Blaisdell turned and looked uncertainly back at Dr. Baird and Nora.

"I'll call you later about dinner," she said awkwardly. "I shall look forward to seeing you."

"That's very kind of you, Mrs. Blaisdell," said Dr. Baird, and smiled.

For a long moment she met his eyes, friendly, warm, and her own fell away, as she nodded and followed Clarissa out of the office and into the warm sunlight to the waiting car.

12

WHEN the car had driven out of the parking area, Nora looked up at Dr. Baird and drew a deep breath, expelling it with a little sigh.

"Well!" she gasped inadequately. "That was quite a session."

Dr. Baird still stood beside his desk, his hands jammed deeply into his pockets, and there was a trace of anxiety in his eyes as he studied her.

"I'm afraid to ask," he admitted frankly, "but I want to know. I don't suppose Dr. Courtney would approve?"

"I haven't the faintest idea what he would have done in your place," Nora said as frankly. "But the results seem to be all that one could wish for. So I'm sure he would approve what you did."

"I'm glad you think so," said Dr. Baird. He dropped down into the chair back of the desk and stared out of the window. "Isn't it queer what crimes can be committed in the name of love? That woman is as sure as anything in the world that she loves her daughter, and so she has done everything she possibly can to ruin the girl's life."

"Being a widow, with only Clarissa to center her life, I'm sure Mrs. Blaisdell felt she was doing what was wise and right," said Nora quietly. "I'm sorry for her."

"So am I," said Dr. Baird unexpectedly. "I'm also sorry for Clarissa, who has been taught that no man could ever love her for herself. What a damnable thing to teach a child! Love is the most necessary emotion any life can hold. Someone to love, someone to be loved *by*—it's the only purpose in life that amounts to a darn."

Nora said impulsively, "With your feeling about love, I wonder you have remained a bachelor for so long."

He looked at her sharply, frowning, and Nora felt the color burn hotly in her face at the realization of the impertinence of the question. And then Dr. Baird grinned forgivingly, and her spirits rose.

"It's because I do feel that love is of primary importance in life that I've remained a bachelor," he assured her, and his tone was one that told her he did not, after all, consider her impertinent. "There are so many counterfeits of love; once you give in to one of those, you're sunk! So it behoves a fellow to be mighty darned sure it's the real thing before he takes the plunge. I've always known that somewhere, at the right time, I'd find my 'true love,' so I haven't been deceived."

Nora dropped her eyes, and her heart tightened. He had been so careful, he boasted; yet surely he had fallen in love with the cheapest, shabbiest of counterfeits of love! Lily Halstead, who looked like every man's dream of love, but who in reality was shoddy and evil. Nora's heart cried out against the thought, but she knew that it was true, and her only hope was that Dr. Baird might learn the truth about Lily before it was too late. She didn't want him hurt! She would have done anything in her power to save him the slightest pain. But of course, there wasn't anything she could do. To try to tell him about Lily would only arouse his protective instinct more fully; deepen his love for Lily, because it would convince him that Lily needed him!

"Are you frightened, Nora?" he asked

quietly, and she caught her breath and looked up at him sharply, appalled at the fear that he had read her mind.

"Frightened?" she repeated dazedly.

"About what Clarissa will do," he said, and Nora breathed again. "Because I can tell you now, with reasonable assurance, that she will stay at home, but that from here on out, she will assert herself and gradually find a more normal life. She threatened to leave, I know; and her mother was panic-stricken. I feel sure that they will talk things over and that Clarissa will remain where she is but that she will never allow herself to be pushed around again by her mother. So you see, there aren't likely to be any unpleasant repercussions to my 'outrageous' behavior today."

"I wasn't thinking there would be," she protested uneasily.

"You looked scared to death," he teased her, and added quickly, "anyway, Dr. Courtney will be home soon, and then he can check up on what's been happening since he went away, and if he's not pleased with my behavior, he can send me packing."

Nora smiled warmly at him.

"I wouldn't be too sure that he'll be home soon," she protested. "He's having a wonderful time. Claims the tourists who go to Florida in the winter time miss all the fun. That it's much better in the summer. He doesn't sound as if he had any thought of coming home for quite a while. Aunt Susie is worried about him."

"Because he's having such a good time?" laughed Dr. Baird.

"She says he'll get into mischief sure," Nora agreed. "But if he was having a miserable time and didn't seem happy, she'd be even more worried. Our family has a great capacity for worrying. We're really experts at it. If we don't have anything really worth worrying about, we always manage to dig up something."

"I always liked the story of the colored woman who said that she always saved up all her worries for Thursday," said Dr. Baird lightly. "No matter what came up on any other day, she refused to worry about it. Then Thursday morning, she got a comfortable chair, put it on the shady side of the porch, settled herself comfortably and worried hard all day! The rest of the time she just enjoyed herself."

"It sounds like quite a system," Nora laughed. "I'll have to tell Aunt Susie about it."

He stood up, glanced at his watch, noting the approach of time for his house calls, and said, as he turned to go, "If nothing important comes up to interfere, why couldn't you and I run in town for dinner tonight, and perhaps see a movie? Would Aunt Susie mind?"

"Of course not," said Nora eagerly. "And I'd love it."

"Good! Then I'll get going and finish up in time to get an early start for an evening out," said Dr. Baird happily, and was off.

Nora sat for a moment beside his desk, after he was gone, savoring the thought of having an evening with him away from the office, from the telephone, from patients. The thought came inevitably, of course: if he had an evening free, as free as a man in his profession could hope to have it, why was he inviting her out, instead of Lily? But she put the thought from her with all her strength. He *had* asked her, instead of Lily, and she was going to make the most of it! And she wasn't going to let herself spoil it by wondering, or even thinking about Lily.

It was a good resolution, and she managed to cling to it while she showered and dressed in her prettiest frock. While she rode beside him to the town's best restaurant and they were given a good table. While they debated happily and hungrily over the menu. But as the waitress departed with their order, Nora turned to say something to Dr. Baird and saw his eyes fastened on the entrance. Startled, she turned to follow the direction of his eyes, and her heart sank with a dull thud.

Lily Halstead stood in the entrance, Jud Carter bending his head above hers devotedly, while they waited to be shown to a table. Lily looked away from him, her eyes sweeping the room, and as she met Dr. Baird's eyes, Nora saw the faintest possible flicker of dismay touch her lovely face. The next instant it was gone and she was saying something to Jud, and leading the way across the room, to pause beside the table where Dr. Baird rose to greet her, his expression enigmatic.

"Hello, Lily, Hi, Carter," said Dr.

Baird, and then to Lily, "Glad your tooth-ache is better."

Nora's heart already lay flat, but now it seemed to grovel. So he *had* asked Lily first and Lily had claimed a toothache! Because, of course, Lily felt Jud was more important to her now than Dr. Baird was but, of course, too wary to let Dr. Baird suspect it.

Lily laughed softly.

"Oh, Mother made me go to the dentist," she said. "I'm such a coward I always have to be dragged to the dentist screaming and fighting every step of the way! And then when I got home, and had rested awhile, I tried to telephone you, Owen, but you were gone. And I was too nervous and upset to stay home, so I called Jud and begged him to take me out."

She looked up at Jud, soft-eyed, sweetly grateful.

"He's such a lamb he didn't mind," she added gently.

"Always happy to be of service to beaut-eous damsels in distress," said Jud, and then, realizing how fatuous that sounded, he glanced swiftly, almost defiantly at Nora, who was merely studying him without expression. "Hi, Nora, you're looking radiant, as usual."

"Thanks so much," said Nora lightly, but her eyes were cool.

"It's wonderful meeting you like this," said Lily gaily, and her eyes took Nora briefly into the scene. "Why don't we have dinner together? It will be so much more fun."

Fun for whom? Nora asked herself sourly, as the men agreed and a waitress bustled about finding two more chairs, crowding the table most uncomfortably. But Lily, cheerfully ignoring the fact, beamed about the table and said happily, "Isn't this nice and cozy?"

Nora said nothing, and Jud shot her a swift, surreptitious glance, even as Dr. Baird agreed politely with Lily. Nora watched, unable quite to deny the admiration she felt for Lily's skill in handling the two men. Both of them were in love with her, both of them must be jealous of the other, yet the scene from the outside was gay and pleasantly informal.

They were half through the rather uncomfortable meal, when Dr. Baird spoke under his breath to Nora, in swift surprise.

"Want to see a metamorphosis? Look who's here."

Nora looked across the room and saw Clarissa Blaisdell, flushed and radiant in a smart, if not too becoming frock, her eyes bright and eager, as she smiled up at the rather weedy-looking youth beside her.

As the waitress guided them to a table, they passed close to that occupied by the foursome, and Clarissa, recognizing them, paused and said eagerly, "Oh, how do you do? Isn't this fun? I'm having a wonderful time—are you?"

Dr. Baird laughed and introduced Lily, and then Jud, who was looking at Clarissa with startled admiration.

"This is Willy Stuart," Clarissa introduced the weedy youth. "I kidnapped him."

"Aw, for Pete's sake," growled Willy, acknowledging the introductions brusquely.

"He brought his mother over to play bridge with my mother and her regular bridge group, so I asked him to bring me out to dinner," boasted Clarissa happily.

"Poor boy, he didn't know how to refuse, and here we are!"

Willy looked down at her, as though puzzled that any girl could get such an obvious kick out of his company, and seemed to grow at least an inch taller.

"I was delighted," he managed, and turned as the waitress spoke. "Our table's ready, Clarissa. We'd better go."

"Don't forget, Dr. Baird, you and Nora are coming to dinner one night very soon," said Clarissa eagerly. She smiled shyly at Jud, and said, "We'd like you to come, too, you and Miss Halstead. Mother will call you."

When she and Willy had gone, Lily looked from Nora to Dr. Baird and demanded flatly, "That's Clarissa Blaisdell. How did you meet her?"

"She is or was, rather—a patient," said Dr. Baird coolly.

Lily's eyes swept to the table where Clarissa and Willy were conferring over the menu and then back to Dr. Baird. Nora told herself she could almost hear Lily's busy brain clicking like mad. The Blaisdells were very top-drawer in Shellville; if Dr. Baird was going to be entertained at dinner in the Blaisdell home, then she, Lily, had been in danger of underrating him. And if by being in a group with Dr. Baird, Lily Halstead could get herself invited to the Blaisdell home, then Lily was going to stay very close to Dr. Baird. Nora felt she could almost see the thoughts racing through Lily's mind.

This, Nora told herself grimly as they were served and began their dessert, was the date with Dr. Baird toward which she had looked with such eager anticipation. And a darned fine date it was turning out to be, with Lily absorbing the attention and the obvious admiration of both Jud and Dr. Baird. Nora found it hard to swallow and was scarcely aware what she ate. It might have been sawdust and herbs for all the taste it had for her.

They were leaving the restaurant when Clarissa came quickly over to them, Willy following her glumly. Clarissa was eager and radiant, her eyes searching their faces eagerly.

"Willy says there's no place we can go and dance on a week night like this," she began breathlessly. "So I thought about the recreation room at home. There's a record player and the floor is smooth and —well, I wondered, if you weren't doing anything special, if maybe we could all go there for a while and dance."

She looked swiftly from one to the other and dark color stained her cheeks, and she added uneasily, "I'm an awful pest, I know, and you've got things planned, so don't mind me—"

Lily glowed eagerly, "Oh, I think that's a wonderful idea! It sounds like grand fun."

Jud and Dr. Baird looked at her, fondly indulgent, and Nora's heart twisted a little more. But of course there was nothing she could say without being a shrew. So they all trooped out to the cars. Willy and Clarissa led, in an expensive, low-slung roadster that made Lily's eyes gleam with jealousy; Dr. Baird and Nora were in his coupé; and Jud and Lily followed. They drove toward the Blaisdell home, which, of course, was in Shellville's most expensive residential section.

Clarissa and Willy were waiting when the other cars parked, and led the way into the wide, beautifully proportioned

189

reception hall, and down the stairs to the basement recreation room.

It was a large room, pine-panelled, with a big fieldstone fireplace at either end. The chairs and wide, comfortable lounges down each side were covered in warm red leather, and the floor was sleek and shining. Clarissa was like a little girl at her first Christmas party, as she skimmed across the room to a large radio-phonography combination, where she paused and turned to them, beaming happily.

"I do hope you don't mind coming," she said swiftly. Their prompt chorus reassured her, as she fitted records on the player, set the control and switched the instrument on.

Jud danced first with Lily, and Dr. Baird with Nora; but soon the party was reassembled and Nora found herself with Willy, who was a smooth, competent dancer not given to the wild flourishes Nora had somehow dreaded and expected. She looked beyond Willy, and saw Clarissa and Dr. Baird seated on one of the long, comfortably cushioned red lounges. Clarissa was flushed and bright-eyed, chattering eagerly while Dr. Baird listened, interested, amused, admiring.

"This is doing Clarissa a whale of a lot of good," said Willy into Nora's ear. "I've seen her around, of course, but I never really got to know her. She's darned near beautiful when she gets excited, isn't she?"

"But there, of course," Nora indicated Lily dancing with Jud, her lovely face lifted to his, laughing lightly, "is the real beauty of this or any other evening."

Willy frowned, as he watched Lily measuringly.

"You think she's beautiful?" he asked as though puzzled at the thought.

Startled, Nora's eyes widened.

"Don't you?" she demanded.

"Oh, she's got the usual number of features assembled nicely and all that, but I don't know that I'd call her beautiful. Matter of fact, she scares me. I wouldn't trust her as far as I could throw a Mack truck, single-handed."

Nora stopped stock-still and stared at him.

"Willy, I love you!" she gasped.

Willy looked shocked and alarmed.

"Hi, now, wait a minute," he protested.

"Oh, it's nothing to frighten you," Nora said, and laughed. "It's just that you're the first man I've ever known who didn't take one look at Lily and fall flat on his face and beg her to walk all over him."

"I bet she does it, too," said Willy dryly. "Looks like just the gal that would love that. But she's not my type, and if she was, I'd change my type."

"Willy, you are a most remarkable man!" said Nora softly.

"Aw, for Pete's sake, just because I can spot a 'phony' when I see one? Heck, a guy learns that before he's out of knee pants," he growled, embarrassed and yet flushing a little as though pleased.

"Some of them don't," said Nora grimly, and flashed a look at Jud, who was so bemused by Lily that though the music had stopped, he was still dancing with her.

"Oh, well, they'll learn. Is Carter your property?" asked Willy frankly.

"Of course not," answered Nora sharply.

"Sorry," Willy apologized. "It was just that I wanted to say that if he is, and Lily's got her claws into him, you really haven't anything to worry about. Oh, sure, she bedazzles a guy, and for a while, he can't see anything but how beautiful she is. But that soon rubs off, like cheap jewelry that turns green so you can see how rubbishy it is. Maybe you're not beautiful, but you're worth a truck-load of her kind, and Jud Carter will find it out and come back. That is, if you want him."

"I don't, thanks," said Nora curtly and then softened to a friendly smile. "But it's nice to know there is at least one man who isn't thrown for a loop when he sees her."

"When you're exposed to her type while you're young," said twenty-year-old Willy in a world-weary tone, "you soon get hep."

Nora smothered her grin against his shoulder, even while she knew that he was right. Willy, son of wealth, must have been exposed to fortune-hunting, predatory women before he was out of grade school and had learned fast. Jud and Dr. Baird were different. Her mouth thinned a little as she reminded herself *how* different they were!

Mrs. Blaisdell's appearance, some time later, signalled the end of the evening. Appearing in the doorway, she looked swiftly about, recognized Nora and Dr. Baird and looked curiously at Jud and Lily.

"Your mother is ready to go home, Willy," she announced. "I heard the music and I do hope you've all been having fun."

Nora almost blinked at Mrs. Blaisdell's cordiality, but Clarissa cried gaily, "Oh, such fun, Mother. This is Lily Halstead, Mother, and Jud Carter. They're coming to dinner, with Nora and Dr. Baird."

"How very nice!" said Mrs. Blaisdell a trifle faintly as though the note of confidence, almost of authority, in Clarissa's voice startled her.

"Will Monday night be all right, Mother?" Clarissa was going to be quite definite about the invitation.

"Yes, of course," said Mrs. Blaisdell graciously. "I shall be looking forward to it."

As they all trooped up the stairs and to the entrance where Willy's mother waited, Nora heard Mrs. Blaisdell say softly to Dr. Baird, "I see I shall have to revise my estimate of you, Doctor. You're a worker of miracles."

"That's very gracious of you, Mrs. Blaisdell," said Dr. Baird pleasantly, and took the hand she extended to him.

Outside, as Willy and his mother drove away, Lily said a blithe goodnight with an especially sweet, intimate smile for Dr. Baird and let Jud put her into his car.

For a moment after Jud had driven away, Dr. Baird stood beside his car, watching until the red tail-light twinkled out of sight, before he turned to Nora and said abruptly, "Well, shall we go?"

"Why not?" said Nora coldly, and got into the car.

13

IT was a few evenings later. To Nora, it had been an almost perfect evening. There had been a letter from Dr. John to discuss during dinner, and afterwards Dr. Baird showed no inclination to excuse himself and hurry away as he usually did. They sat in the living-room and played canasta, while Aunt Susie busied herself with her thoughts and her crochet.

It was close to eleven when Aunt Susie said firmly, "Well, you children can stay up over that silly game all night if you like, but I'm going to bed."

Dr. Baird said lightly, "Sounds like a good idea. And anyway, I've won this game, and I really fought for it. I'm not taking a chance on getting licked by playing another. You're really good, Nora!"

Nora's heart was warm with the happiness of the evening, and she laughed gaily. "Oh, it's nothing, really! Only don't ever play poker with me. I'm an expert at that —Grandfather taught me."

"Thanks for the warning!"

"Would you like something to eat?" suggested Nora, loath to end an evening that had been so quietly happy.

"After that dinner?" Dr. Baird grinned. "Well, perhaps a glass of milk and a cookie. I'm a growing boy, judging by my appetite, anyway."

"Eating at this hour of the night? You won't sleep a wink," protested Aunt Susie fondly, and went on up the stairs.

Nora and Dr. Baird were at the kitchen table, drinking milk, eating cookies, relaxed and enjoying themselves, when the telephone in the hall shrilled.

"Oh, no, not at this hour of the night," Nora wailed as she rose to answer it.

Dr. Baird grinned at her. "It's merely the shank of the evening, my girl, in a doctor's day, as you should know."

She lifted the receiver, and spoke briskly. A woman's voice, shaken with grief and agitation, stammered in her ears, and she recognized Mrs. Halstead's voice.

"Oh, Nora, please come right away. Mr. Blayde has had some sort of attack," Mrs.

Halstead babbled. "I know Dr. Baird is out somewhere with Lily, but I haven't any idea where to get in touch with them. And, Nora, I'm frightened. Please, *please* come."

"Of course," said Nora instantly, and dropped the receiver into its cradle.

Dr. Baird was beside her, and she explained swiftly, "It was Mrs. Halstead. Mr. Blayde has had an attack."

Dr. Baird was reaching for his worn, familiar black case, heading for the door, even as he answered crisply, "I've been afraid of that. Let's go."

Mrs. Halstead had said that he was out with Lily. That, of course, meant that Lily had lied to her mother and no doubt was out with that unpleasant-looking character called Eddie. For a moment, as they jumped into Dr. Baird's car and drove towards the Blayde's home, she was tempted to tell him what Mrs. Halstead had said, but she swallowed the words and her peace.

There were lights downstairs in the Blayde home, and in the big corner suite that was Dick Blayde's personal quarters. A servant swung the door open even as the car skidded to a stop, and Nora and Dr. Baird leaped out and went hurrying into the house.

Mrs. Halstead was halfway down the stairs, her face white and strained, her eyes brushed with terror that faded as she saw Dr. Baird.

"Oh, thank goodness you found him, Nora!" she panted in such acute relief that her words did not seem to register on Dr. Baird's mind, already preoccupied with the patient, as he went swiftly up the stairs and to Dick Blayde's room.

Nora, following hard on his heels, knew the moment she looked at the gaunt, gray-faced man who lay unconscious, that the Angel of Death hovered in the room. It was a presence she could sense, almost she could feel it. And though Dr. Baird went swiftly to work, she knew that he, too, realized it was too late.

It was not more than an hour later, though all three of them had lost track of time, when Dr. Baird laid the thin bony wrist beneath the covers and straightened, his expression telling Mrs. Halstead that the man who had befriended her and her child was gone.

She gave a small, strangled cry of such heartbroken woe that Nora turned quickly and put her arms about the woman, drawing her out of the room and back down the stairs. She urged Mrs. Halstead into a chair, and tried to soothe the wild sobbing. A little later, Dr. Baird was there, preparing an injection that would help to calm the grief-stricken woman. Nora assisted him swiftly, and after a moment, Mrs. Halstead relaxed very slightly and looked at them with wide, bleak eyes.

"I don't know how to thank you, Nora, for coming, or for finding Dr. Baird and bringing him with you," she said huskily, her voice thick with sobs. "I know it was terrible of me, but I couldn't bear to be alone with him, and unable to help him. He's been so good, so kind. I'll never forget his goodness to Lily and me."

Dr. Baird said gently, "Would you like me to attend to the arrangements, Mrs. Halstead? Notify his family, his relatives?"

"He has no relatives, Dr. Baird. That's what makes it all so heart-breaking. There is no one in the world to grieve for him except Lily and me, and the servants."

Mrs. Halstead broke down again and sobbed.

Nora heard the sound of a car outside, and then running footsteps along the verandah, and Lily burst into the house. Flushed, bright-eyed, extravagantly lovely.

"What's up?" she demanded as she ran into the room, and her eyes widened as she saw her grief-strickened mother. And then she looked swiftly, suspiciously at Dr. Baird and Nora. "I saw the house all lit up and I stopped to find out—"

She bit back the words, and caught her breath.

"It's Uncle Dick, of course," she said after a moment. "He's worse, isn't he?"

"Oh, darling, he's dead!" wailed Mrs. Halstead.

Nora, watching Lily, felt sickened by the look of avid eagerness that touched Lily's lovely face.

"No kiddin'?" she asked softly. "He really *is* dead?"

Dr. Baird said curtly, "Quite dead!"

Nora looked up swiftly at him, and set her teeth hard against the look of bitter pain and shock in his eyes as he watched Lily.

For a moment Lily stood quite still, and then she threw back her lovely head and laughed aloud. An ugly, raucous laugh that must have struck unbelievably on Dr. Baird's ears, accustomed to that soft, silvery chime of bells that was the laughter he had heard from her before.

"So he's really gone at last!" Lily couldn't keep the wild triumph out of her voice: "The old so-and-so finally kicked off! And I'd begun to be afraid he'd live forever—or until I was old and ugly anyway!"

Something indescribably evil seemed to have come into the room with the girl. Nora had known of it, of course; Mrs. Halstead and Dr. Baird had not. Now they stared at the girl as though they had never set eyes on her before.

Lily laughed again, and suddenly she went whirling about the room, dancing, kicking high until her pale-rose organdie skirts were like a bell above her dancing feet.

"So the old boy is really dead!" she cried. "And I'm free to get away from this fly-speck of a town and never set eyes on it again! Free while I'm still young and beautiful, and I'll have money to do anything I want to do!"

Mrs. Halstead was white and sick with horrified protest.

"Lily! How can you say such awful things! You're out of your mind," she wailed.

Nora dared not look at Dr. Baird, and her hands were clenched tightly into fists as she watched the flushed, radiant girl whose beauty seemed to have slipped away so that now she was ugly and loathsome.

"Out of my mind? I am, Mother, I really am. Out of my mind with delight and excitement," cried Lily. "Because do you know what the old dodo left me in his will? Twenty-five thousand dollars! Jud told me!"

Nora caught her breath in shocked protest.

"Jud violated Mr. Blayde's confidence?"

Lily gave her a contemptuous one-sided grin that twisted her mouth into unlovely lines.

"I told you I could make him do anything I wanted him to," she drawled maliciously. Her eyes brushed Dr. Baird's white, set face and her contempt for him added to her malice. "I can make any man do anything I want him to, can't I, darling?"

As she said it, the word was an epithet, and Nora thought she saw Dr. Baird flinch. But he did not speak, and Lily said, suddenly remembering. "Oh, I forgot. Eddie's waiting for me. I'll have to tell him the good news and send him on his way. Because of course now that I've got all that money, I don't want to be bothered with a cheap rat like Eddie. He *is* a rat, of course; but he's been fun. And he seemed to have money to spend, which is more than can be said of some of the other men I know."

The ugly laugh floated behind her as she ran out of the room.

Mrs. Halstead was all but hysterical with shock and grief. Dr. Baird and Nora got her settled in her room, sleeping beneath the kindly opiate before they left her. As Nora came down the stairs, she heard Dr. Baird at the telephone.

"Carter?" he was asking, and then he went on, "this is Owen Baird. I believe you are attorney for Richard Blayde? Then you should know that he passed away a

204

short time ago. I imagine that there are instructions in his will as to the necessary arrangements? Oh, you will? Good. Then I'll leave all that to you. Mrs. Halstead went to pieces from shock and I've given her a sedative, so I'm afraid you'll have to take over."

When he put down the telephone, Nora was at the foot of the stairs, and he looked up at her swiftly, his face a taut, dark mask.

"She's sleeping quite comfortably," said Nora gravely. "I'll come back in the morning and bring Aunt Susie. There are friends who will see her through this."

"Then we may as well go," said Dr. Baird, and held open the door for her.

He said nothing as they drove back home. And then as they went into the house she turned impulsively and, before she could check her words, said, "I'm terribly sorry."

"About Blayde?"

"Of course, but I wasn't meaning that. I meant about Lily."

"Thanks." His tone was grim, and then, to her surprise, his eyes narrowed and he demanded sharply, "You knew she was like this, all along, didn't you?"

As though the suppressed anger in his voice had been a blow, she took a backward step and dark color poured into her face.

"Well, answer me. Didn't you?"

"I've known Lily for years," she admitted unhappily.

"But you never tried to warn me?" There was accusation as well as pain in his voice.

"That's not true," she flashed hotly. "I did, when you first came, and you practically bit my head off."

He made a gesture of defeat and nodded.

"I suppose so," he agreed wearily. "A fool and his folly—I'm beginning to sound like a Grade B-minus movie, come to think of it. Forgive me, if you can—and isn't this where you laugh?"

"I never felt less like laughing in my life," she told him quietly.

His eyes brushed her briefly as he went past her and up the stairs, and his words fell back to her. "Thanks. That's very kind of you."

14

WHEN she came down to breakfast in the morning, Aunt Susie said anxiously, "Owen must have had an early call. He drove away about six o'clock and without even a cup of coffee."

Nora tensed, then quietly told her aunt of the death of Mr. Blayde, and of the ugly scene that followed when Lily had discovered his death.

"The nasty little brat!" said Aunt Susie grimly. "Still, I don't know that anybody should be surprised, except that for once she'd slip and let people guess what's behind that loveliness of hers."

"Dr. Baird was surprised," said Nora, and even in her misery could have laughed aloud at the inadequacy of the understatement. "He was shocked and just about heart-broken."

Aunt Susie stared at her.

"Well, for heaven's sake, why should he be heart-broken?"

Nora looked at her in weary surprise.

"You didn't know that he is madly in love with her?" she asked dryly.

Aunt Susie's eyebrows went up and her eyes beneath them were startled and protesting.

"Nonsense, he couldn't be such a fool," she protested. "Jud Carter, now—of course I knew she was leading Jud around by the nose. But surely Owen couldn't have been taken in by her."

"That's where you are badly mistaken, pal," said Nora grimly.

Aunt Susie studied her uneasily for a moment.

"But I thought you—that is, I mean I thought he—" Her voice stumbled to abashed silence as Nora glanced at her and then away.

"You were wrong," said Nora curtly.

"I'm sorry, darling," said Aunt Susie quietly.

Nora managed a taut smile.

"Oh, I'll get over it," she drawled.

"Maybe." Aunt Susie was obviously not convinced.

There was the sound of a car in the drive, and they tensed as Dr. Baird came in. His face looked drawn and haggard, as though he had not slept, but his manner was cool and calm.

"I stopped by to see Mrs. Halstead," he told them as he accepted gratefully the cup of coffee Aunt Susie held out to him.

"How is she, poor soul?"

"She seems to have felt it deeply; it's obvious that she had a great deal of gratitude and honest affection for the old man," said Dr. Baird. "I thought perhaps if you could, you might run over and comfort her. She is very fond of you."

"Of course. I'll go immediately," said Aunt Susie. Irrepressibly she asked, even while Nora glared at her, "Of course Lily is with her?"

Dr. Baird shot a swift, angry glance at Nora, and his voice was taut when he said, "I wouldn't know. I didn't see Lily."

Nora excused herself and left the room, hurrying toward the small office. She could not endure sitting there across the table and seeing Dr. Baird's taut, withdrawn look, and her heart was twisted with bitter loathing for the girl who had hurt him so.

His manner, when he came to the office

for the morning hours was as usual. The days slid by, and neither spoke of Lily or of that evening. But late one afternoon almost a week after the funeral, Jud telephoned Nora, who was alone in the office.

"Mr. Blayde's will is being read tomorrow afternoon at two," he told her curtly. "You and Dr. Baird are supposed to be there."

"But for goodness sake, why?" protested Nora, puzzled.

"You'll find out," said Jud dryly. "Just see that you're both here."

The telephone clicked and Nora stared at it, bewildered. She was still sitting there, looking puzzled, when Dr. Baird came back from his house calls.

His preoccupation vanished as he saw her face. Frowning, he asked quickly, "Is something wrong?"

Nora looked up at him.

"I don't know," she admitted, and added hastily, "oh, nothing is wrong. At least I don't suppose it is. Jud Carter called and said Mr. Blayde's will was being read tomorrow afternoon."

Dr. Baird's jaw tightened.

"She's not losing any time, is she?"

"Did you think she would?" Nora flashed, and added before he could answer, "Jud wants us to be there for the reading of the will, but he wouldn't say why."

Dr. Baird's eyebrows went up.

"Both of us?" he asked incredulously.

"That's what he said. And when I asked why it was necessary, he just gave a sort of bark and said, 'You'll find out. Just see that you are both here.' It's to be at the Blayde home."

Dr. Baird shoved a hand in his pocket and ran his free hand through his already tousled hair, and his brows were drawn together.

"Only those whose names are mentioned in a will are expected to be present," he mused aloud. "I can understand, of course, your name being in the will, but it's ridiculous to think I'd be mentioned. Dr. Courtney, yes; that's to be expected. But me? I barely knew the man."

"It's equally ridiculous to think he would remember me," Nora began.

Dr. Baird smiled at her faintly.

"Why? The old man was fond of you, Nora. You had been kind to him and he was very lonely," he said gently. And then he made a gesture of dismissal. "Oh, well, silly wondering about it. This time tomorrow we'll know. Were there any calls —I mean aside from Carter's?"

Nora offered him the slip containing the calls, he thanked her and went on into his office, and the afternoon followed its usual pattern. After dinner, Dr. Baird excused himself and went to his room, carrying several medical journals and magazines that had arrived in the day's mail, and Nora sat alone in the living-room, for Aunt Susie had already gone to bed.

Her thoughts were not pleasant company, and she was glad when there was the sound of a car in the drive. She sprang up to unlatch the screen door and then stood back, startled, as Jud came in.

"Well, this *is* a surprise." She could not keep back the words.

"Don't kick me out. Nora," he begged, grinning ruefully. "I know you should, but—darn it, I've missed you like the dickens."

"I've been right here," Nora pointed out dryly.

"So you have," Jud admitted, abashed. "Only I've been so busy making a fool of myself I guess I just sort of forgot. Could I, please ma'am, come in? I'm a big boy now, house-broken and everything."

"Of course," said Nora, and smiled at him. "After all, better men than you have been fooled by golden curls and limpid blue eyes."

"Ain't it the truth?" Jud agreed grimly. "Doc Baird, for instance."

"And a minor-gangster type named Eddie, as another instance," Nora reminded him, and led the way into the living-room, waving toward a chair, curling herself in another near it. "You look very tired, Jud. Is it mental or physical?"

"Both," admitted Jud. "With a thick smattering of self-disgust. Nora, how in blazes can a girl manage to look like Lily and yet be such a monster?"

"Girls are funny people sometimes, Jud!"

"Yeah, and men are complete fools most of the time," Jud agreed. "Of course, no gent ever low-rates a lady; but then I never claimed to be a gent, and the beauteous Lily is no lady, so maybe the rule doesn't hold."

There was a brief silence, and then Jud looked up at Nora. He was leaning forward in his chair, elbows on his knees, his hands loosely locked together. His eyes had been on his hands, but now they were upon Nora, with something like an ashamed plea in their depths.

"When I think how I was taken in by that gal, to the extent of betraying the confidence of a swell old gent like Mr. Blayde, I could shoot myself," he said grimly. "I could be disbarred for it, too, and I should be."

"She's pretty persuasive, Jud, and very lovely," Nora pointed out.

"Oh, sure," he agreed, his eyes once more on his hands. "I understand she put on quite an act when she found that Mr. Blayde was dead."

"It was a vicious, callously brutal scene that I shall never forget," admitted Nora thinly.

"She was at my office the next morning when I got there, demanding the will be filed for probate that morning and read that afternoon before the funeral," said Jud, and Nora shivered. "We had quite a set-to, incidentally. I guess I got as good a view of the girl-behind-the-lovely-exterior as Dr. Baird. It wasn't pretty."

"I can imagine," said Nora quietly.

There was a brief silence, and then Jud looked up at Nora.

"I suppose I'd be wasting my breath if I asked you to forgive me?" he hazarded at last.

"Forgive you, Jud?" she protested, honestly puzzled. "For what?"

"For making a fool of myself about her. Everybody around town that we knew must have thought I was passing you up for her." Jud stumbled awkwardly in his efforts to make himself understood. "Of course you and I know it wasn't true. I mean, that we had ended our understanding, that never was an engagement anyway, before I started seeing Lily."

Before Nora could speak, he made a little hushing gesture, and added quickly, "I'm making a mess of what I'm trying to say, Nora, which is only that I'd like us to be friends again, if you can forget what a heel I've been."

"I never stopped being friends with you, Jud," Nora protested warmly. "And once Lily set out to capture a man, the man doesn't have much chance. I understand how it happened."

Jud grinned at her warmly, in sharp relief.

"That's the nicest thing anyone has said to me in a long, long time," he told her swiftly. "Thanks, Nora."

"For nothing," Nora dismissed it quickly.

"I'll toddle along then." Jud rose. "I'll expect you tomorrow at two, in the library at the Blayde place. You and Dr. Baird."

"I told him you were expecting us, but neither of us have the faintest idea why," admitted Nora frankly.

Jud grinned tautly. "Don't ask me to violate my client's confidence again, Nora. Once was plenty."

"I had no intention of asking it!" she told him swiftly.

"I'd probably do it, if you did," said Jud. "I seem to be a pretty funny sort of lawyer. Maybe I'd better get into some other profession where a fellow isn't supposed to keep secrets!"

Irrepressibly Nora said lightly, "Or else be more careful about your girl-friends."

Jud nodded grimly.

"Don't worry about that," he told her. "I've learned my lesson."

"Then you have nothing to worry about," Nora assured him.

He looked down at her for a moment thoughtfully.

"You're quite a girl, Nora," he said levelly. "I'm just beginning to realize how swell a person you are, now that it's too late for the knowledge to do me any real good."

Nora stood up and for a moment laid her hand on his.

"Look, Jud," she said quietly, "you and I knew some time ago that we had made a mistake about the way we felt toward each other. Remember?"

"Sure." Jud nodded not too happily. "I remember. You gave me my walking papers, but good, and I don't blame you for a moment. You're a pretty wonderful girl, Nora, but I have brains enough to know you're not for me. You never really were, come to think of it. We just sort of got into the habit of believing we were 'meant for each other,' if I may coin a phrase!"

Nora nodded soberly.

"That was it, Jud. And I think maybe you sort of fell for Lily on the re-bound, or am I flattering myself?" She smiled unexpectedly.

"You're flattering me, and being very kind, and I'm grateful," Jud told her, and turned toward the door. "Well, I'll be seeing you and Owen tomorrow afternoon."

"I'll be there, since you make such a point of it that you have aroused my curiosity," Nora told him. "But I can't promise about Dr. Baird."

Jud paused, and his brows drew together.

"You mean he's not coming?"

"I don't know, Jud. I gave him your message but I can't promise you what he'll do about it. He's not talking much nowadays."

"Is he in?"

"Upstairs in his room."

"Then maybe I'd better run up and have a word with him," said Jud. "Because the will can't be read unless he is there, and I shudder to think what Lily would do if the will were not read! Seems she's in a terrific dither to be going places."

Without waiting for Nora's answer, he went quickly up the stairs, and she heard the sound of his knock at Dr. Baird's door, and his voice saying, "Open up, Owen. It's Jud. I'd like a word with you —maybe two or three!"

She heard Dr. Baird's door open, and then close behind Jud. She waited with a curious tenseness until Jud came down, perhaps ten minutes later.

"He'll be there," he said from the doorway, grinned at her, lifted his hand in a little half-salute and was gone.

15

THOUGH the shades were drawn, excluding some of the heat, the big library was hot and close. Not a breath of air stirred in the garden beyond the open windows. The room was well-filled, and Nora was surprised at the extent of the staff of servants that had looked after Dick Blayde and the big house. They sat in chairs along the back of the room, tense and waiting, murmuring now and then, hushing their voices guiltily the next moment as though they were in church.

Mrs. Halstead, care-worn, her face blotched with weeping, sat wearily in a deep chair, and Nora, in a sleeveless, thin frock, knew that Mrs. Halstead's unrelieved black must make her extremely uncomfortable in this heat. Lily was also in black; but it was a thin, sheer black with elbow-length wide sleeves and a demure white organdie collar at the high neck-line. With her golden curls tucked into a demure knot at the back of her head, with the beauty of her exquisite young body artfully enhanced by the severe cut of her frock, Lily was even more devastating than usual. She had not demurred about wearing black, of course; it was too becoming to her fragile blonde loveliness for her not to jump at the chance.

When Nora came in, the last of the expected group, there was a small rustling and settling as the servants relaxed and made themselves as comfortable as their eager expectancy permitted. Nora did not look at Dr. Baird as they seated themselves near the door, and she did not know whether he glanced at Lily or not. But her eyes were on Lily, and she saw that Lily seemed aware of nobody in the room but Jud.

Jud, seated behind the big handsome desk, had a somehow touching dignity, as though he had acquired it from the importance of his task. He glanced around the room, saw that they were all settled and waiting, and unfolded the bulky blue-bound closely typed sheets that lay before him.

The will began with the customary

assurance that it had been made when its testator was in sound mind and complete possession of all faculties, and then it went on with various legacies to the servants, all of whom had been with him for several years or longer. Now and then a servant sobbed, or gasped as the amount left to him or to her was read aloud.

"To my faithful friend and devoted housekeeper, Mrs. Jerome Halstead, the sum of fifty thousand dollars," Jud read and heard Lily's startled gasp and Mrs. Halstead's sob, "which is invested in a manner to give her a comfortable and assured income for life. At her death, should the investment be intact, it is to be returned to my estate for handling as outlined below. But should she wish to have the cash, my administrators are instructed immediately to dispose of the stock in which this amount is invested, and to hand her the entire amount, tax-free, in cash."

Lily leaned forward eagerly, urgently, whispering to her mother, who turned a shocked, indignant face upon her and pushed her away with a gesture of such sharp negation that Lily's face darkened with anger.

Jud waited deliberately until Lily was once more facing him, and then he went on reading, his tone without expression, colorless.

"To Lily Halstead I leave the sum of twenty-five thousand dollars in cash, tax-free and with no strings or conditions attached," he read, and Lily gave a little ecstatic crow of delight as though hearing it read from the will itself gave her the necessary extra assurance that Jud had told her the truth when he had betrayed Dick Blayde's trust in him.

"To Nora Courtney," Jud read, "who has been kind and gentle to a tired, sick old man, and who is one of the finest, most honest girls I have ever known, I leave the sum of five thousand dollars, knowing that if I made it a larger sum, she would either decline to accept it or turn it over to charity. It is my earnest wish that Nora use this money to buy a lot of frivolous, extravagant things such as every young girl wants and should have."

Nora could not control the tears that slipped down her cheeks and was startled when Dr. Baird, smiling at her, patted her hand lightly and then offered his handkerchief which she accepted with a slightly damp smile.

Lily shot her a spiteful, maliciously triumphant glance, obviously gloating in the fact that her legacy was five times that of Nora, and then she looked back sharply at Jud.

"Well? What about the rest of it?" she demanded. "Uncle Dick must have been worth a million at the very least. These legacies are only chicken-feed. What's he doing about the house and grounds and all the rest of the estate?"

Jud eyed her for a moment, and Nora cringed for Lily at the look of contempt and loathing in his eyes.

"It is my wish," Jud read from the will in answer to Lily's sharp question, "that my home and the grounds be made into a hospital, for which it seems to me ideally suited. A hospital where the sick and ailing, without regard to race, creed or color, may receive the best of medical treatment and care, regardless of whether they have money to pay or not.

"I, therefore, leave the balance of my

estate, when the above legacies and all necessary expenses have been attended to, to Dr. Owen Baird."

Dr. Baird's sharp exclamation of surprise and protest clashed with Lily's angry cry, but Jud silenced them both with a stern look and went on with the will.

"Having great confidence in Dr. Baird, not only as a thoroughly competent and capable physician, but also as a man of integrity and character, I have no hesitation in leaving the whole estate in his hands. The estate will provide ample funds for the conversion of my home into a hospital, and my stock in the mills and other income-paying investments will provide the necessary endowments. I therefore with great pleasure and complete confidence in Dr. Baird name him as the sole heir to my entire estate, exclusive only of the legacies mentioned above."

Jud's voice was drowned out by Lily's furious protests, and he raised it so that the final words of the will could be heard above her furious anger. And then he dropped the will on his desk and watched Lily coolly.

"Of all the filthy, lousy, low-down tricks," Lily was crying out, while the servants looked at her with cold distaste and Mrs. Halstead stared at her as though she had never seen this dark-faced girl before. "The stinkin' old so-and-so! I work myself to death looking after him and waiting on him hand and foot and enduring his foul temper and insults; then he leaves me a beggarly little twenty-five grand, and more than a million dollars to a doctor he barely knew!"

She whirled on Dr. Baird, who was watching her with a curious intentness that made Nora quail slightly, so disgusted and contemptuous was it.

"You have no right to it, darling." Lily tried hard to keep her voice down to its warm, coaxing level. "So of course you're not going to accept it, are you? You know it should belong to Mother and me. Because you've done nothing to earn it and we've slaved for him for years. So of course you'll refuse it, since you aren't entitled to it?"

Dr. Baird smiled slightly, but it was neither a pleasant nor a friendly smile.

"Why, no, Lily, I'm not entitled to it,"

he began, and she whirled toward Jud without waiting for him to finish.

"You see? Owen's not going to accept it, so doesn't that mean Mother and I get it?" she demanded sharply.

"You didn't let me finish, Lily," said Dr. Baird coolly. "Of course I'm going to accept it, with deep gratitude and appreciation."

Lily whirled upon him, her filmy skirts swinging above her lovely ankles.

"But you just said you were not entitled to it," she cried sharply.

"I'm not," Dr. Baird drawled. "But the people of Shellville and the surrounding area are. Those sick and ailing, without regard to race, creed or color, who may or may not be able to pay for needed medical treatment are entitled to it, and if it comes to them through a bequest left to me, I shall accept it as a sacred trust."

Lily stared at him as though she could not force herself to believe that he really meant it. For a moment he met her eyes coolly, and then he turned to the servants, who were rising, starting to leave the room.

"I know that some of you have been

here a long time," he said pleasantly. "No doubt you feel at home here and perhaps you would like to stay on. Of course no arrangement can be made as yet, but I am sure that any of you who wish to remain can do so. Perhaps, Jud, a month's salary while we get things adjusted and see what's to be done?"

"Sure, Owen, you're the boss now," said Jud, and grinned.

"Then we'll let things stand as they are for the present, and you can all have time to decide whether you'd be willing to stay on and work in a hospital." Dr. Baird let the servants go with a friendly smile. As they left the room, there was a cheerful babble of voices as they discussed the matter.

Dr. Baird turned to Mrs. Halstead and took her hand, patting it lightly, comfortingly.

"As for you, Mrs. Halstead, I'm sure you know how happy I'd be to have you stay on as my good right hand, unless you feel the work would be too much for you," he said gently.

Mrs. Halstead's tears flowed, but they were tears of relief as her words revealed.

"Oh, Dr. Baird, I've so hoped you'd feel like that ever since I first knew what Mr. Dick planned," she wept gratefully.

Lily, who had been watching and listening unbelievingly, gasped in sharp outrage, "You knew he was planning this, Mother?"

Mrs. Halstead bridled, and her eyes on her daughter were cool.

"Of course," she said loftily. "He discussed it with me from the first. Originally, he planned to leave it to Dr. John, but when he talked it over with him, Dr. John told him frankly it was too big a job for a man his age, and that he would much prefer Dr. Baird should do it."

Lily was dumbfounded.

"And you, my own Mother, never tipped me off!" She gasped.

"Mr. Dick trusted me," said Mrs. Halstead simply.

"And you let me make a fool of myself, and get cut off with a lousy twenty-five thousand dollars, when I could just as easily have played my cards right and married Dr. Baird!" Lily burst out hotly.

Dr. Baird stiffened, and Jud grinned wryly at him. For a moment it looked as though Owen meant to make some savage answer; then he turned to Nora and said politely, "Shall we go?"

Jud stood up and said cheerfully, "We'll get together on all the details, Owen, as soon as you're ready."

Dr. Baird nodded an acknowledgement, and while Lily started after him with dazed, blindly furious eyes, Nora walked beside Dr. Baird out of the room and into the hot sunshine where his car waited.

Nora turned and looked back at the handsome yellow brick house and then out over the sweep of lawn and trees and gardens.

"It will make a wonderful hospital," she said quietly.

Dr. Baird nodded as he helped her into the car.

"It scares me," he admitted frankly. "Oh, it's what every doctor dreams about, and few ever realize. But it's a terrifying responsibility."

"Oh, I'm not worried about that," Nora assured him quite sincerely. "You'll swing it. I know you will."

Before he started the car, Dr. Baird

looked down at her curiously as though seeing her for the first time. And then, as he started the car, he said, "Thanks, Nora, thanks a lot."

16

AS he parked the car in the area in front of the small white office, Nora saw that the door was open, and that though there were several cars parked, there were no patients visible.

"Why, I'm sure I locked the door before we left," she gasped.

"Of course you did. I saw you," said Dr. Baird, frowning, as they both got out of the car and moved swiftly to the door.

From inside came the sound of eager, laughing voices, and as Nora and Dr. Baird stepped into the reception room, they saw the group of patients surrounding a man whose back was to them. He wore cream-colored slacks and a violent-colored Hawaiian sports shirt, short-sleeved above brown elbows, and when he turned, they stared for a moment, not quite recognizing Dr. John. He seemed to have dropped off years as he had dropped off pounds; he was leaner, hard and bronzed and laughing, as he accepted the tribute of their astonishment.

"Darling!" gasped Nora, and flung her arms about him, while the patients looked on in warm approval. "I could have met you in the street and not recognized you! Why, you look like a kid!"

Dr. John kept an arm about her, gripped Dr. Baird's hand and said, a twinkle in his eyes, "I've always had my doubts about that Fountain of Youth we've been hearing about for years; but it's true. I found it."

Dr. Baird said lightly, "That's obvious, sir. You look it. But I don't think I'll call you 'sir' any more. There's not enough difference in our ages for me to get away with it."

Dr. John beamed happily at him, and Nora asked eagerly, "When did you get back, darling?"

"Half an hour ago," said Dr. John. "I came, of course, as soon as I got Susie's letter about Dick Blayde. I was very sorry to hear of it, though of course I had more or less expected it."

He looked sharply at Dr. Baird, his eyebrows asking a question and slipping back into place as Dr. Baird nodded. He became conscious then of the waiting patients and excused himself to go on into the private office.

At the door, Dr. Baird paused and looked back.

"Coming, sir?" he asked.

"Certainly not," answered Dr. John forcefully. "You've got along without me this long; think I'm going to step back into harness again? Not on your life!" He turned to the waiting patients and grinned. "You lucky people!"

There was fond laughter, and Dr. John seated himself and began talking to an elderly man, while Nora and Dr. Baird went briskly about the business of attending the patients one after the other. By the time the last one was gone, it was time for Dr. Baird to start on his house calls, and once more Dr. John refused vigorously to accompany him, and remained with Nora when Dr. Baird had gone.

Nora sat very still, looking after Dr. Baird's car, momentarily forgetful of Dr. John's wise, probing eyes.

"Like him, don't you, baby?" he asked very quietly.

Color poured into Nora's cheeks and she could not quite meet his eyes, though she kept her pretty chin high.

"Of course," she responded. "Everybody does. He's a very good doctor. Right now, he admits he's a little scared."

Dr. John nodded slowly.

"Blayde's bequest, eh?"

"He feels it's a terrible responsibility."

"That's the way he should feel, because it is. But Blayde and I were both convinced that he could handle it. It won't be a one man job, of course, but just the same being the head of the place is going to keep him jumping. But don't you worry, baby, he can handle it."

"Well, who's worrying?" Nora snapped. "Of course he can. I never for a moment doubted it."

Dr. John's wise, kind old eyes were studying her shrewdly.

"And of course you'll be there to help him," he said gently.

Nora caught her breath and the color fled from her face.

"I shan't—" she protested.

Dr. John was never one to beat about the bush, and he had only scorn for any sort of evasion.

"You mean you're not in love with him?" he demanded.

Nora's head was high, but in spite of her attempted control there was a mist of tears in her eyes.

"Of course not," she insisted valiantly.

"Poppycock! You never could lie convincingly, and you're an idiot to try it with me," snapped her grandfather. "You're crazy about him, so don't try to kid your old grandad."

Nora said quietly, "OK, so I'm crazy about him. And a heck of a lot of good it's going to do me."

Dr. John bristled indignantly.

"Do you mean that young fool hasn't got sense enough to appreciate you? That he's not in love with you?" he demanded incredulously, anger sharpening his tone.

"Not by several million miles, darling." Nora managed a light if not too convincing laugh.

"Then maybe Blayde and I were wrong about him," growled Dr. John. "Maybe he's not as smart as we thought he was."

"Don't be ridiculous, darling. Not falling in love with me doesn't disqualify him from being the head of a fine hospital."

"No, but it does sound as if he were lacking somewhere."

Nora was silent for a moment, and then she said wearily, "Oh, well, I thought maybe Aunt Susie might have had time to tell you."

"Your aunt had time to scream my name, assure herself I had survived my first airplane flight without injury, and departed at a gallop for the super-market, as if there was never any food in the house unless I was home," Dr. John told her.

"Well, then, you may as well know. Dr. Baird sort of got side-tracked from any other girl when he met Lily Halstead," Nora told him bluntly.

Dr. John's bushy white brows were drawn together in a puzzled frown.

"You mean he was fool enough to be taken in by that bonbon candy-box look of hers? Then he *is* a fool," he snapped.

"In that case, there are a lot of masculine fools around town," Nora assured him sharply. "You ought to know that as well as I do. Lily's pretty devastating."

"'A pretty face with naught behind it,'" Dr. John quoted one of his favorite comic-strip characters.

"I suppose so," Nora agreed reluctantly.

Dr. John was silent a moment, and then he chuckled.

"I suppose when she found out that Dick Blayde had left the bulk of his estate to Owen, Lily collapsed in his arms, batted those long lashes of hers and bleated 'My hero!'" he drawled.

Quietly, Nora related the story of the night Dick Blayde had died, and Dr. John listened, anger growing in his eyes as he visualized the scene.

"So when she found out he was the fair-haired boy in Blayde's will, it was too late for her to make any hay with Owen," he said with enormous satisfaction. "Oh, well, a fellow should recover eventually from a blow like that."

"Eventually." Nora's emphasis was grim.

They sat in silence for a moment, and then Dr. John asked, "Things been going all right? Folks around here take to Owen as their doctor?"

"They like him tremendously, but of course, your own patients will welcome you home again," Nora assured him, smiling warmly.

"Ha—they should live so long," snapped Dr. John, and Nora stared at him, wide-eyed.

"Do you mean you're not resuming practice?" she demanded.

"We'll talk about that later," Dr. John told her, and stood up. "I see Susie's back, so I'll go up to the house and get her started on dinner. See you then."

He strode out, and Nora watched him as he went up the walk toward the house. Exulting in the way he held his shoulders back, and the youthful stride of his walk. Remembering the way he had looked when he had gone away only a few months before, looking tired, his shoulders bent, like an old man, she could rejoice in the obvious good his vacation had done him. It was so good to have him home again. She had missed him more than she had realized until this moment.

At dinner, Dr. John held forth at enthusiastic length on the beauties he had encountered on his vacation, and the wonders of Florida.

"I tell you, Susie, it's a fantastically beautiful place," he told her. "You know these pot-plants you get so excited about and nurse along so eagerly? What do you call 'em? Begonias?"

"Cast no aspersions on my cherished begonias!" Susie said sternly, her eyes fond of him.

"Down there, folks use 'em the way people use petunias up here," Dr. John assured her. "Great beds of them growing all over the place. Use 'em to border walks with. The poinciana trees are something you have to see before you can believe a tree could be so beautiful! The jacaranda is really a sight, too. And there's a night-blooming cereus that looks like green snakes coiling around thick-bodied trees, until suddenly along in June and July it starts blooming. Folks who know them can take a look at a bud—and the buds are the size of electric light globes—and tell you within minutes just what time that night it will bloom. Susie, my girl, you're going to be crazy about it."

Aunt Susie stared at him, wide-eyed.

"*I'm* going to be crazy about it?" she repeated.

Uncle John glared at her.

"Well, certainly. You're going back with me, of course."

Aunt Susie gasped, "I'm going back with you?"

Dr. John banged his fist on the table.

"For Pete's sake, stop making like a parrot and repeating everything I say," he snapped.

"Don't yell at me!" ordered Aunt Susie, her voice low and controlled, her eyes snapping.

"Then don't make me so gosh-darned mad!" Dr. John yelled.

Anxiously Nora stole a glance at Dr. Baird, fearful that he might be embarrassed, or take them seriously. But Dr. Baird's eyes held a twinkle and he was trying hard not to grin, and as his eyes met Nora's he winked at her, sharing his amusement with her. And Nora, relieved that he understood these beloved two so well, smiled warmly at him until she saw the twinkle got out of his eyes and a new, startled warmth come into them. She felt color burn in her face and turned once more to Aunt Susie and Dr. John, who were quite unaware of the brief byplay and who were still glaring at each other.

"You mean to tell me you're going back to Florida?" demanded Aunt Susie.

"You don't think, after seeing what it's like down there, I'd be willing to spend any more time here than I could help, do you?"

Aunt Susie studied him.

"I told you if you went off like that by yourself you'd make a fool of yourself," she told him witheringly. "And now look at you—running around in slacks, for Heaven's sake, and that awful shirt, and not even tucked into your pants. A man your age running around with his shirt-tail hanging out!"

Dr. John stiffened.

"It's the way all the men dress in Citrus City," he told her haughtily. "The weather is hot and the men have sense enough to dress comfortably."

And before she could answer that he chuckled.

"You won't be down there a week before you'll be running around in sun-back, sleeveless dresses, or a playsuit, maybe even shorts!" he warned her cheerfully.

Aunt Susie bridled indignantly.

"I should see the day!" she snapped, as though he had made an outrageous suggestion.

"I will, it's a foregone conclusion," Dr. John assured her, grinning. "But it's really a wonderful place, Susie. You'll love it. The house is small—two bedrooms, a combination living-room and dining-room and a kitchen that's straight out of a 'home beautiful' magazine. Of course I didn't get any furniture. I wanted you to select that. But there is a garden planted, and space for a kitchen garden. Though it's farming country and fresh vegetables are so cheap it hardly pays you to raise them. The lake is so full of fish that they almost crawl up on the bank and beg you to catch them. There's wonderful game, too, if a fellow likes to hunt. Why, drat it, you can almost live off the land! We've got a couple of orange trees for shade in the patio and we can have more." He stopped as Aunt Susie waved a feebly silencing hand.

"John, for pity's sake, you sound delirious," she protested. "Are you trying to tell me you've made all your arrangements to go back down there to live? Permanently?"

Sulkily, Dr. John nodded. "That's what I've been trying to tell you ever since I got home. But it seems to take a long time for a thought to percolate that gray head of yours."

Aunt Susie looked at him helplessly, and then despairingly at Dr. Baird and Nora.

"He's out of his mind," she gasped faintly. "At his age, and mine, we're supposed to pull up stakes and go down to this crazy place to 'live off the land.'"

"Nothing of the sort," snorted Dr. John, outraged. "If you'd just keep still long enough for me to say a few words—"

"I ask you, Nora and Owen, a few words indeed! Who else has been able to get a word in edgewise since he got home?" she all but wailed.

"What I have been trying to say is that there hasn't been a doctor in Citrus City since the young one was drafted into the armed services early in the spring," Dr. John stated coldly. "It's twenty miles to the nearest doctor, and the Chamber of

Commerce and business people there were quite excited when I drove in town and they saw the caduceus on my car. I had a number of patients, even if I didn't even have an office. The drug-store fixed me up a room in which I could see my patients, and they have made me a very attractive proposition: one that a man of my age, who wants semi-retirement, would be a fool to turn down. I admit it might not appeal to a young, up-and-coming man who is ambitious and wants to go places; but for an old codger like me who wants just enough work to do to keep him out of mischief, it's ideal. And I told 'em I'd be back just as soon as I could get things cleared up around here. The house I was telling you about goes with the job. And if you don't want to go back with me, dang it, I'll find me a housekeeper!"

Aunt Susie drew a deep breath and her eyes were wide with astonishment and growing excitement.

"Then there really *is* something to all this!" she breathed.

"Well, what in blazes have I been trying to tell you?" he snapped.

"Oh, you were raving along so I thought

you just had a touch of Florida fever," Aunt Susie assured him, and now her eyes were shining. "Of course we'll go back with him, won't we, Nora?"

Dr. John said hurriedly, "Well, I'm not sure Nora would like it. It's an old folks' paradise. Now don't get riled, Susie; maybe I should have said middle-aged folks. But it's not much of a place for a young girl like Nora."

Nora stared at him, deeply hurt.

"So I'm to be turned out of the only home I've ever known, just because I'm not middle-aged?" She tried to make her tone sound gay, but hurt was in her voice.

"Honey, I never for a moment thought you'd care about going." Uncle John so carefully avoided looking at Dr. Baird that Nora turned scarlet. "The bungalow down there only has two bedrooms, and there's not enough work for a nurse for you to keep your hand in, and most of the folks are middle-aged and the young people don't seem to hang around long after they get old enough to get ambitious."

"If Nora doesn't go, then I don't go," snapped Aunt Susie fiercely. "How

246

dare you make plans that don't include Nora?"

"Well, I suppose I just sort of took it for granted Nora had plans of her own," Dr John said hastily, and still kept his eyes from Dr. Baird, who was now acutely uncomfortable, his eyes on his plate.

"I have, of course, darling," said Nora swiftly. "Now that I'm practically a rich woman, I'll go to Atlanta and take an apartment and maybe a job as a 'luxury nurse' and live a life of ease."

Dr. John said uneasily, "Well, of course I knew what Blayde had in mind, and I guess I took it for granted that maybe you'd like a job in the hospital here."

Before Nora could answer that, Dr. Baird said swiftly, "There will always be a job for Nora at Blayde Memorial Hospital, any job she wants."

Nora had herself in hand now and could smile gaily at all of them.

"Thanks a lot, but I think I'd like to try Atlanta for a while. There are always a lot of exciting things going on there and it should be fun. I knew some Atlanta girls in training there, and some of the internes should have gathered and set up shop by now, so I won't have any trouble landing a job," she assured them. "And you two youngsters get yourselves busy getting ready to take off for Florida."

For a moment Aunt Susie looked at her carefully, almost pityingly, and Dr. John smiled at her fondly and said quietly, "You know I'm only kidding when I say I made no plans for you. There's always a plan in the old duffer's heart for his baby."

Nora drew a long hard, uneven breath and blinked the mist from her eyes.

"In a minute you'll have me crying, and that's not fair," she scolded him. "Tell us more about this Garden of Eden you've found."

"That's about what it is," said Dr. John happily, and once more launched forth on his enthusiastic story.

Nora listened, feigning a bright, eager interest and trying very hard not to be conscious of Dr. Baird's set, dark face as he sat looking down at his untasted dessert, not seeming to be listening at all. Nora knew that Dr. John had taken it for granted that by the time he came home she would be engaged to Jud Carter and so there need be no plans for her. It was a thought that would have made her laugh except that the tears were so close she dared not risk it.

17

THERE had been, for almost a year, a standing offer for the Courtney property by an ambitious Shellville real estate firm that wanted to turn it into a tourist home for travellers. There was room on the grounds for half a dozen cabins, and the two-room office building would be perfect for an office. The price offered was a generous one, and Dr. John closed with the firm, promising possession, completely furnished except for Aunt Susie's most treasured "bits and pieces," at the end of thirty days. Which flung Aunt Susie into a dither of packing, choosing, deciding what she absolutely could not part with, and the inevitable cleaning.

Dr. John had agreed to help Dr. Baird get the Blayde Memorial Hospital in shape before he left. There was so much to be done, what with patients requiring attention, that Nora was almost too busy to think and deeply relieved that this should be so. At night, Dr. Baird and Dr. John were deep in discussions, plans, poring over the necessary equipment, frequently calling on Nora for help. And Aunt Susie, now and then bursting into tears of excitement and frustration, needed Nora's soothing advice in deciding just which of her cherished belongings would fit most adequately into the Florida bungalow and the new life she would live there.

All of Shellville was excited and stimulated by the news of Dick Blayde's legacy. Civic-minded laborers, contractors, building material people offered rock-bottom prices for what was needed, and the work moved with a speed that would not have been possible on a purely private enterprise.

Lily had departed for New York, insufferably stuck-up, Nora's friends reported, over her inheritance, and talking importantly about what she was going to accomplish.

"According to her," Aunt Susie announced, after returning from a party given by one of her numerous clubs, "she'll be Miss America by Labor Day. I'd hate to tell you what I think she'll be."

"Aunt Susie! Don't be spiteful!" protested Nora half heartedly.

Aunt Susie sniffed.

"I'm only repeating what everyone at the party said," she insisted, and looked lovingly at Nora. "Are you sure, darling, that you don't want to go with John and me to Florida?"

"Quite sure, lamb," Nora assured her firmly. "Now that I know you two are going to be all right, and don't need me to keep a watchful eye on you, I'm going to step out and carve a career for myself. Does that sound selfish?" she interrupted herself anxiously to ask.

"Selfish? You?" Aunt Susie gave a lady-like snort. "You couldn't be selfish if you tried; you don't know how!"

She hesitated a moment, and Nora looked at her sharply.

"You're keeping something back, Susie," she said with mock sternness. "You're wasting your time, trying it. You know I can read you like a book. So come on; out with it. What else was discussed at the sewing circle?"

"It wasn't the sewing circle; it was the Book Review Club," Aunt Susie protested innocently. "The sewing circle is giving a party for me day after tomorrow. And much as I appreciate it, I wish they wouldn't, because I just haven't time for any more parties."

"Come on," Nora insisted, eyes twinkling. "Give! What's the rest of the gossip?"

Aunt Susie turned away from her for a moment and spoke over her shoulder uneasily.

"Are you still in love with Jud Carter, darling?"

Nora stared at her, wide-eyed, completely astonished.

"Of all the silly questions! Of course not. I never really was. I just thought I was."

Aunt Susie turned anxiously, worriedly.

"You're sure? He didn't—well, jilt you because of Lily?"

Nora hooted inelegantly.

"Look, pet, if there was any jilting done —which there wasn't—I did it!" she said firmly. "Marsha, bless her, offered us her life's savings so we could get married immediately. And that opened my eyes to a truth I had never faced before: namely, that I didn't really want to marry Jud. We had drifted into an understanding sort of by force of habit. So he and I talked things over and faced facts, and that was that."

She studied Aunt Susie for a moment, and then, a hint of uneasiness in her voice, she asked quickly, "What's happened? Is Jud in some sort of difficulty?"

"You'd be upset if he were?"

"Well, silly, of course I would. Jud and I have been friends all our lives and I'm very fond of him, almost as though he were my brother." There was complete convincing sincerity in Nora's voice, and Aunt Susie smiled with relief.

"Then it's all right to tell you, because you'll have to know it sooner or later, and I guess you would already have heard if you hadn't been so busy helping Owen and John get the hospital thing all straightened out."

Nora laid her hands on Aunt Susie's shoulders and gave her a small, stern shake.

"Come out from behind that bush and stop beating around it," she ordered. "And tell me what you're trying to say."

"It's just that Jud has been seeing a lot

254

of Clarissa Blaisdell and everybody is quite sure that Mrs. Blaisdell will announce their engagement any minute." Aunt Susie spoke with a swift rush of words as though it was a great relief to get them spoken.

Nora's eyes widened and there was color in her cheeks.

"Well, isn't that wonderful?" Her delight was so sincere, so warm, that Aunt Susie relaxed and beamed at her. "What an ideal match! Why, they're perfect for each other. Clarissa is a darling, and she needs somebody like Jud to help her develop that new personality."

"Then you don't mind?"

"Mind? Why you silly darling, I'm tickled to pieces!" said Nora happily. "I'm wondering if Mrs. Blaisdell will try to throw a monkeywrench, though. They're scandalously rich, and she may have ideas about a suitable husband for Clarissa."

"Apparently, she is delighted," said Aunt Susie. "She and Marsha have become friends. Marsha and Jud are frequently there for dinner, and Clarissa and Mrs. Blaisdell come to tea with Marsha. It all seems to be working out beautifully."

"That's wonderful!"

Aunt Susie looked at her anxiously and then smiled.

"Then I can go ahead and tell you the rest of it," she said happily.

"There's more?" Nora teased, laughing.

"Marsha has invited us to dinner tomorrow night," said Aunt Susie. "You and Dr. Baird and me. And Mrs. Blaisdell and Clarissa will be there and do you know, I wouldn't be a bit surprised if Mrs. Blaisdell announces the engagement!"

Nora nodded, but before she could speak Aunt Susie rushed on.

"So I want you to go straight downtown and buy yourself the prettiest dress you ever owned! And hang the cost!"

Nora laughed. "Darling, that's silly. My yellow crepe will be quite festive enough, and besides, I haven't time to go shopping."

"I stopped at Gleason's on my way home from the party and selected three dresses in your size, any one of which would be perfect on you, so all you have to do is run down, make your selection and bring one home. I'm sure they won't have to be altered, because you're a perfect size," Aunt Susie assured her breathlessly. "And you've simply got to look your prettiest, darling. If you don't want to, for your own sake, do it for John and me. We want to see just how beautiful you *can* look, now that you can shop without even having to look at the price tags."

Startled, Nora said, "Why, I can, can't I?"

"Of course you can, and it's what Mr. Blayde wanted you to do, Nora. You will, won't you?" begged Aunt Susie anxiously.

"Well, if it means so much to you, yes I will," Nora agreed. "But the thing I felt I needed most, now that I shall be working in Atlanta, is a good little car. If I'm going to be a private duty nurse, I'll need good transportation."

"I wasn't supposed to tell you," admitted Aunt Susie, "and John will probably strangle me for spoiling his surprise. But he's giving you a new car, out of the money he's getting for the place."

"But he mustn't do that. You'll need that money," protested Nora.

Aunt Susie grinned lovingly.

"It will do you no good to argue, because he and I selected it yesterday and it's to be delivered in two days. And if you let John know I tipped you off in advance, I'll spank you! He wants it to be a surprise. And after all, it's the least we can do after abandoning you like this, and literally selling the roof right over your head!"

"Don't you worry. I'll be so surprised I'll fall flat on my face with joy when he drives it up," Nora promised. "And abandoning me my foot! Look, I'll make you a promise. I'm a big girl now and it's high time I got out and shifted for myself. But if the going gets tough or I get scared, I'll hop in the new car and make a beeline for Florida and throw myself on you again."

Aunt Susie beamed happily. "Well, I've never yet known you to go back on a promise, so if you'll make that promise then I won't worry about you any more," she said. "And now, scat downtown to Gleason's and get that dress, you hear me?"

"That I will, darling, that I will," laughed Nora, and hugged her warmly. . . .

Both Dr. John and Dr. Baird protested at the dinner invitation, but Aunt Susie was unexpectedly stern and unexpectedly firm. So at last, growling a little, Dr. John gave in.

"We won't have to stay long," he comforted Dr. Baird grumpily. "And Marsha sets a fine table."

"And it will give you an opportunity to meet one of Owen's patients I think you really should know, darling," said Nora firmly. "A girl who was being smothered to death by maternal authority, and so completely crushed that she was in danger of a genuine physical illness. It would have done your heart good, I know, to have heard Owen read out the law to Mrs. Blaisdell, and to see how Clarissa has emerged from her repression. She's a darling."

Dr. John flung her a swift glance, and then looked back at Dr. Baird, who grinned disarmingly.

"It was nothing, really," he tried to disclaim. And then, seriously, he went on. "The girl was on the verge of a complete breakdown, mental as well as physical. And when I realized what a steam-roller her mother was, I guess I gave her the rough side of my tongue. I'm afraid you would not have approved, though."

Dr. John's bushy eyebrows rose.

"Worked, didn't it?" he demanded.

"It seems so."

"Then I approve," said Dr. John firmly, and eyed Dr. Baird with added respect.

18

AUNT SUSIE adjusted the folds of
Nora's filmy white tulle frock and
stepped back, nodding eager
approval of the slender, graceful body
enclosed like a flower-bud in the snugly
fitted sequined off-the-shoulder bodice,
with the skirt billowing mistily above
silver slippers.

"I'm so glad you chose this one, Nora,"
she said happily. "It was the one I liked
best, but I didn't tell you so because I
didn't want to influence your choice. You
were never more beautiful in your life.
Though I never saw you when you weren't
beautiful."

She sniffed, blew her nose vigorously
and said, "Well, come on. Don't stand
there admiring yourself. We're late as it
is."

Nora laughed and hugged her, and they
went down the stairs together to where Dr.
Baird and Dr. John awaited them. Aunt
Susie, in silver-gray satin, looked

distinguished and handsome. She was a foil to Nora's white-and-sequined splendor, and the two men stared at her, startled by her blossoming.

Nora looked into Dr. Baird's eyes and saw the astonished delight there, but the next moment his eyelids had dropped and he was making some pleasantly flattering remark to Aunt Susie.

"You two go ahead in your car, Owen," said Aunt Susie briskly. "John and I will follow in mine. Then if there should be a call for you, though I devoutly hope there won't be, of course, you won't be bothered by having to bring us home."

"Them's orders, them is," said Dr. John dryly. "I'm wondering how I'm going to put up with her, once the two of us are alone down there in Florida. She'll ride me ragged, without Nora to take up for me."

"It's high time somebody bossed you around," Aunt Susie said serenely, but her eyes on him were warm and tender and his own returned the affection.

"You mean I haven't been bossed by you since the day I was born?" was the best he could manage by way of any answer.

Nora and Dr. Baird went out to his car, and as he helped her into it he said lightly, "Too bad I didn't know an angel straight from the top of a Christmas tree was going to ride with me tonight. Maybe I could have found time to have the car washed. Country roads are always either inches-deep in dust or foot-deep in mud, it seems, and whichever it is has a fatal affinity of a medic's form of transportation."

"Well, of course, that's something I'd never have suspected, since my knowledge of country roads and medics's means of transportation is so limited." Nora tried to sound gay and flippant.

"Get going, you two," called Dr. John behind them, and Dr. Baird grinned and started the car.

It was the first time she had been alone with him, away from the constant interruptions of the office, since the reading of Dick Blayde's will. Nora tried to deny her feeling of shyness, telling herself how utterly ridiculous it was, and searching her mind desperately for some gay chatter to break the tension.

"Have you any idea what we may hear tonight at dinner?" she asked him gaily. "Or are your ears closed to town gossip?"

She knew instantly by the slight tautening of his jaw that he had heard.

"You mean that rumors are winging all over town about Jud and Clarissa?" he asked quietly.

"Yes. Isn't it wonderful? I think they'll be very good for each other, don't you?" said Nora happily.

For a moment he looked down at her sharply.

"You are not upset?" he probed.

"Why should I be? Jud's my good friend, almost like a brother, and I've come to know and like Clarissa a lot these weeks since she's been consulting me about such vitally important things as hair-dos, make-up and becoming colors and fabrics."

Her voice was cool, serene, perfectly composed, and she was startled to hear him release a held breath.

"Did you think I'd mind?" she asked him frankly.

"Well, I knew, of course, that you and Jud had been practically engaged when I

264

first came to town, and I wasn't sure that that was all over. Not really over, I mean," he answered cautiously.

"It has been for some time," she told him.

He hesitated a moment and then he asked quietly, "May I ask an almost unforgivably personal question?"

"Of course," she answered instantly, and then added, "because if it *is* personal, I shan't promise to answer it."

"Fair enough," he agreed, unsmiling. "It's just this: was it Lily who broke up your engagement to Jud?"

"Of course not," she answered him so swiftly, so honestly that he could not but believe her.

"That's a relief," he said as honestly. "You're such a wonderful person, Nora. You're worth a hundred Lily Halsteads. I would find it very hard to endure if I knew that she had had any effect whatever on your life."

Nora hesitated a moment, and then she said evenly, "Lily had nothing whatever to do with my breaking off with Jud. It was just that he and I both realized we were not really in love, that we had just sort of drifted into an engagement and that the only sensible thing to do was to call it off and start over again with someone else. And I'm terribly pleased and happy that Jud has found his love. Clarissa is a darling."

"Yes, Jud's a lucky guy. A man who finds his love always is, if his love is returned," said Dr. Baird, and there was something so close to grimness in his tone that Nora gave him a startled glance. But they had reached the Carter home now, and Dr. John and Aunt Susie were climbing out of their car and joining them, and there was no further chance for the conversation.

The Blaisdells' Cadillac was already parked, with the uniformed chauffeur lounging at the wheel. When Aunt Susie and Dr. John, followed by Dr. Baird and Nora went up the steps and to the door, it swung open and Jud greeted them happily, Clarissa at his elbow. Nora looked swiftly from one to the other. There was such warmth and love in Clarissa's eyes as she looked proudly at Jud, and Jud's touch was so gentle when he reached for her hand and presented her to Dr. John, that

Nora's heart warmed for both of them. They were two people deeply and joyously in love and it was very good to see them so.

"Nora, darling." Clarissa's voice rang with happiness. "Aren't you beautiful?"

Nora laughed warmly.

"No, but you are," she answered gaily.

Jud beamed at her and then at Clarissa.

"The two most beautiful gals in Shellville," he said proudly. "We're a couple of lucky guys, Owen. When we march into the Country Club tonight, there won't be a man who won't envy us."

"Are we marching into the Country Club?" asked Dr. Baird pleasantly.

"Sure. After dinner," said Jud. "The others are going to play bridge, but we are going dancing."

"Sounds like fun," Dr. Baird agreed cautiously.

They were in the living-room now, being greeted by their hostess and by Mrs. Blaisdell, who shook hands warmly with Dr. Baird, and under cover of the gay hubbub of greetings said quietly, "I am deeply grateful to you, Dr. Baird. I hope you will let me express my gratitude by equipping a room at the hospital or in any other way that may seem good to you."

"That's very kind of you, Mrs. Blaisdell," said Dr. Baird. "And I'm happy to know you have forgiven me."

"I only hope you can forgive me, and that some day Clarissa may," said Mrs. Blaisdell huskily.

"I don't think there's room in Clarissa's heart for anything but her happiness, do you?" asked Dr. Baird gravely.

"I hope not," admitted Mrs. Blaisdell. "Jud's a fine boy. They are insisting that they live on his income, but they are going to let me make them a wedding present of a little house. I'm glad of that. But I promise you, Dr. Baird, I'll keep my hands off their lives."

"I'm sure you will," Dr. Baird told her, "because I'm sure that you have never wanted anything for her but her own happiness. It's just that it's sometimes very hard for parents to see their children make mistakes, and to realize that's the only way they can grow up. Mistakes are a part of life. A not very pleasant part, perhaps, but inevitable."

Dinner was announced and they all

trooped into the dining-room. Sensibly, Marsha had not attempted an elaborate party such as she knew Mrs. Blaisdell was accustomed to. She had planned and prepared the dinner herself, and it was simple, deliciously cooked and the sort that any maidless hostess plans so that she may spend the maximum of time with her guests.

There was laughter and bright chatter throughout the meal, and when they were dawdling over coffee and Marsha's famous lemon chiffon pie, Mrs. Blaisdell looked about the group and smiled, though there was a mist of tears in her eyes and the smile was faintly tremulous.

"I don't expect any of you to show the slightest surprise at my announcement," she said lightly. "It's an open secret, but it's part of the routine to make the formal announcement. Therefore, I ask you all to rejoice with me in the announcement of my daughter's forthcoming marriage to Judson Carter. And may they live happy ever after."

Clarissa turned to Jud, radiant, and put her hand in his. The others offered congratulations and good wishes, and Mrs.

Blaisdell and Marsha exchanged misty-eyed smiles and that was that.

Half an hour later, the four young people were trooping out to the cars, and the four older people were settling down for a game of bridge.

Jud put Clarissa tenderly in his car, blandly ignoring the Cadillac at the curb, and drove away. Dr. Baird smiled down at Nora and swung open the door of his car. She settled herself contentedly, and he slid beneath the wheel.

As the car swung out of the drive and took the direction along which Jud and Clarissa had driven, Nora sighed and leaned her head back and looked up at the sky, silver-washed with stars so thick and so bright they obscured the blue of the heavens. The moon was late and had not yet peeped above the horizon, yet the star-shine made the scene so tremulously light that it was almost like moonlight.

"It's wonderful to see two completely happy people, isn't it?" She sighed. "I'm so terribly glad for them."

"So am I," said Dr. Baird, and after a moment he said quietly, "I shall miss you very much, Nora, when you go."

"Thanks, it's nice to know that," Nora told him as quietly. "I'll miss you, too, and all my other friends here, and my home town."

"You will until you get settled into a new life in a big city like Atlanta," he said almost grimly.

"I'll never get so settled I won't miss Shellville."

Dr. Baird was silent for a moment, and then he turned his head and looked down at her.

"This may be the last chance we will have, Nora, to talk alone before you go." His tone made her heart leap like a puppet on a string. "Are you in a terrific rush to get to the Club and the dancing?"

"Of course not," said Nora, and then blushed because she had spoken so swiftly. "It's early yet, barely nine-thirty."

"Good," said Dr. Baird. "There are some things I want to say. I know they won't be in the smallest degree important to you, Nora, but they are to me. I'd like to have things clear between us before you go; and then if you aren't happy in Atlanta, you'll feel free to come back to

271

Shellville, to Blayde Memorial if not to me."

Her heart gave a small lurch, and she looked up at him. But it was dark in the car, despite the silvery starshine, and in the faint light from the instrument panel she could tell nothing of his expression. She sat tensely beside him, her hands locked in her lap, and she dared not try to answer him for fear her voice might betray the agitation in her heart.

Ahead of them a small, meandering path turned at right angles from the highway, and Dr. Baird turned the car into this, off the highway, and stopped it. He switched off the ignition and turned to her, and for a moment there was no sound in the summer night save that of the tiny insects in the tall grass on either side of the narrow road.

"It's never easy for a man to confess that he has made an utter and complete fool of himself, Nora, but sometimes it's good for him," he began awkwardly. "I know it isn't going to make a single scrap of difference to you, or alter your plans in the least; but I'd like you to know that I now realize the complete and disgusting folly of my brief infatuation for Lily. Oh, it was wearing thin even before that night when she knew Mr. Blayde was dead. Even if I had been wildly and madly in love with her still, that love would have been utterly destroyed by her brutal revelation of her emotions. But because it *was* wearing thin, I knew that moment that she was cheap and selfish and rotten. I had already found out that she was spoiled, selfish, and that the truth wasn't in her. I was puzzled to know why I could have been fooled by her even for an instant; but I admit that I had been fooled and that I richly deserved my punishment. One that will last as long as I live."

Nora sat very still for a long moment, and then she managed to bring her voice up and out enough to ask shakily, "Your punishment?"

He did not look down at her. His hand moved restlessly on the wheel, and his eyes were on the star-lit field beyond them.

"Finding my love when it was too late," he said grimly. "Being blinded by Lily's beauty and synthetic charm to the truth that you were the one girl I could ever really love or want to marry."

Nora held her breath, her teeth sunk hard into her lower lip, her hands clenched tightly.

"You are entitled to hoot with derision at me, Nora," he went on painfully. "I suppose if I'd had enough pride, I'd have kept it to myself and let you go away, without ever letting you know that, now the cobwebs are out of my mind and my heart, I know that I love you and that I'll go on loving you as long as I live."

Still she was silent, and Dr. Baird glanced down at her, a pallid ghost of a girl in the darkness beside him, and leaned forward to switch on the ignition.

"Isn't this where you laugh in my face and tell me to get going, straight out of your life? I shan't blame you, because I deserve it and I know you could never have anything but contempt for me," he finished.

"You fool!" Nora whispered, her voice shaking, barely loud enough to reach his tensely listening, straining ears. "You utter fool!"

"I am, of course; isn't that what I've been confessing?" he asked harshly, and her hand shot out and closed over his before he could turn the key in the ignition switch.

"That's not what I meant," Nora murmured, and her hand was clenched tightly over his, that turned instinctively to grasp it. "I meant you were a fool not to know that I've been crazily in love with you almost since the first time I saw you!"

She heard him draw a sharp, incredulous breath as he turned swiftly to her, and even in the duskiness in the car she could see the white, strained look of his face even as she heard the tenseness of his voice. Yet all he could say was her name, in a shaken voice that made it a question whose answer he was afraid to hear.

"Didn't you understand, darling," there were tears in her voice but it was triumphantly ringing, "that people can't quarrel the way you and I did at our first meeting, unless they are deeply interested in each other? If they're not, quarrels aren't important; if they are, then they seem to try as hard as they can to say the ugliest, meanest things—because it's the people we love who can hurt us the most."

"Nora," he said, and his voice was low,

shaken, "are you by any chance trying to tell me you have forgiven me?"

"For Lily and for thinking you loved her?" she demanded, and now her voice was more steady, touched with healthy anger. "Well, Lily's a sort of disease that has affected practically the entire male population ever since she was sixteen. But it's not an incurable disease and it doesn't last long, thank goodness!"

Dr. Baird waited, and Nora swayed toward him, her face lifted. His arms went about her and caught her close, and held her as though he meant never to let her go again. And as she gave herself to his embrace his kiss on her mouth was the most perfect, the most wonderful experience she had ever known. Her cool, soft hands framed his face between them, and she gave him back his kiss with an ardor and an enthusiasm that made his heart vibrate like a violin in the hands of a master violinist.

For a long, long moment, or it may have been an hour, neither knew nor cared, they held each other close, and then Dr. Baird drew away from her just far enough so that he could look down into her shining eyes.

"Nora, how soon will you marry me?" he begged.

Nora was silent for a moment, and her silence made a quick stab of terror into his heart. He gave her a tiny shake.

"Nora," his tone was urgent, "you *are* going to marry me?"

Nora laughed richly, joyously.

"Well, of course I am, silly," she told him lovingly, and emphasized it with a kiss. "I was just thinking. It would scarcely be legal unless Aunt Susie and Grandfather were present, and they're leaving Sunday! That only gives us three days, but then I never believed in long engagements, did you?"

"Oh, my precious darling," said Owen huskily. And though his voice was low, and broken with yearning tenderness, it had in it the exultation of a ringing shout, the exultation of a man who sees the gates to his most cherished private paradise swinging open before his eyes.

We hope this Large Print edition gives you the pleasure and enjoyment we ourselves experienced in its publication.

There are now more than 2,000 titles available in this ULVERSCROFT Large print Series. Ask to see a Selection at your nearest library.

The Publisher will be delighted to send you, free of charge, upon request a complete and up-to-date list of all titles available.

Ulverscroft Large Print Books Ltd.
The Green, Bradgate Road
Anstey
Leicestershire
LE7 7FU
England

GUIDE
TO THE COLOUR CODING
OF
ULVERSCROFT BOOKS

Many of our readers have written to us expressing their appreciation for the way in which our colour coding has assisted them in selecting the Ulverscroft books of their choice.

To remind everyone of our colour coding—this is as follows:

BLACK COVERS
Mysteries

*

BLUE COVERS
Romances

*

RED COVERS
Adventure Suspense and General Fiction

*

ORANGE COVERS
Westerns

*

GREEN COVERS
Non-Fiction

ROMANCE TITLES
in the
Ulverscroft Large Print Series

The Smile of the Stranger	*Joan Aiken*
Busman's Holiday	*Lucilla Andrews*
Flowers From the Doctor	*Lucilla Andrews*
Nurse Errant	*Lucilla Andrews*
Silent Song	*Lucilla Andrews*
Merlin's Keep	*Madeleine Brent*
Tregaron's Daughter	*Madeleine Brent*
The Bend in the River	*Iris Bromige*
A Haunted Landscape	*Iris Bromige*
Laurian Vale	*Iris Bromige*
A Magic Place	*Iris Bromige*
The Quiet Hills	*Iris Bromige*
Rosevean	*Iris Bromige*
The Young Romantic	*Iris Bromige*
Lament for a Lost Lover	*Philippa Carr*
The Lion Triumphant	*Philippa Carr*
The Miracle at St. Bruno's	*Philippa Carr*
The Witch From the Sea	*Philippa Carr*
Isle of Pomegranates	*Iris Danbury*
For I Have Lived Today	*Alice Dwyer-Joyce*
The Gingerbread House	*Alice Dwyer-Joyce*
The Strolling Players	*Alice Dwyer-Joyce*
Afternoon for Lizards	*Dorothy Eden*
The Marriage Chest	*Dorothy Eden*